# A CROWN OF WILD MYRTLE

The setting of this novel is a small
Greek island, at the height of summer. An Englishman travelling alone
makes the aquaintance of a girl,
Ruth Forbes, and her older travelling
companion, Mrs Keller. It soon
strikes him that the relationship between the two women is not merely
an uncomfortable one; it has in it
something ominous; indeed it is sinister. He gradually discovers that the
girl is, in fact, being held in a sort of
emotional bondage.

How he succeeds in releasing her
from this bondage and in giving her
the kind of love she very desperately
needs forms the theme of a tale that
is near-tragic in its suspense and
ominous beauty.

# ALSO BY H. E. BATES

# H. E. Bates

## A CROWN OF
## WILD
## MYRTLE

*London*
MICHAEL JOSEPH

*First published by*
MICHAEL JOSEPH LTD
*26 Bloomsbury Street*
*London, W.C.1*
1962

*Set and printed in Great Britain by Tonbridge Printers Ltd,*
*Peach Hall Works, Tonbridge, Kent, in Baskerville twelve*
*on fourteen point, on paper made by Henry Bruce at Currie,*
*Midlothian, and bound by James Burn at Esher, Surrey*

# I

'I tell you there *were* cockroaches.' Once again the voice of the girl came with brittle tension through the port-hole from the deck immediately above. 'Why on earth should I invent cockroaches?'

The *San Philippa*, old, shabby, high out of the water, had a single smoke-stack like a tall coal-black candle. As she slogged her way from one Greek island to another, up through the hot Ionian sea, the sound of engines thumped and thundered in her bowels like the beat of an ancient pumping station. The inlaid satinwood of her cabins had long since faded to a dirty amber; the rickety sash-windows of her port-holes rattled gloomily in the night. Her dining saloon was a hot dark dungeon aft, panelled in fumed oak, its air thick with old odours of engine oil and onions. There you paid only for such food as you wanted to eat, merely to discover that you didn't want to eat it after all.

Jack Marsden, who was travelling by himself and had woken soon after first daylight, put out of his mind all thoughts of an impossible breakfast, then dressed and went up on deck to discover that the ship was tying up in an airless, sparkling little bay beautifully land-locked between great flanks of sun-parched mountain. A quayside crowded with people and lined with flat-roofed houses exactly like toy building blocks in pink and blue and white and peppermint-green lay under high slopes of olives and lemons, mulberries and cypresses, occasional bananas and many fig-trees. Great rose-bay oleanders smouldered everywhere over trailing vines.

For a few minutes he stood watching with fascination a man loading several acid-green coils of narrow hose-pipe on to the back of a mule as if they were snakes of pure gold. From time to time the muleteer stroked them with positive affection and finally strapped them down with two lengths of scarlet and white harness that buckled under the belly-band. Then an open car filled with many stoical old ladies with heads tied up in handkerchiefs of various colours drove at reckless speed along the waterfront, scattering everything from donkeys to dogs, and with equal fascination Jack Marsden watched that too. The only things that didn't scatter were a pair of early lovers partly entwined about a blue and silver bicycle against a hot white wall and partly about each other.

'I tell you there were cockroaches. I simply couldn't sleep. I sat up on deck all night.'

'To you everything that crawls on the floor is a cockroach.'

'Don't be so sarcastic.'

'To you anything in the nature of a scrap of truth is sarcastic.'

'Don't be so impossibly preachy. It doesn't suit you early in the morning.'

'Correct me if I'm wrong—but the original idea of boarding this crawling Victorian tub in the first place was yours, not mine. Now suddenly you read in the papers that war is going to break out any moment and you're scared. Plain scared. And being scared always makes you ill-tempered.'

'I am not scared. I am not ill-tempered. It's merely that if there's going to be a war I'd rather be back home in Baltimore.'

'Of course you're scared. You were even scared of the cockroaches that were never there.'

A flounce of white went past Jack Marsden like an angry, signalling flag. He had a brief glimpse of a woman of forty or so in a white shirt and white duck shorts of impossible width, her hands stuck with fury into the pockets. A moment later he was left staring at a girl of twenty-five or so beating her hands in speechless vexation on top of the taffrail. Her hair, of a curious peachy blonde shade, curled fluffily on her neck and her face and arms were sun-burned to a deep shade of brown that looked almost artificially brilliant against her turquoise blouse and the sherry colour of her linen slacks.

The brittle quarrel over the sudden rumour of war completely baffled him. War, for him at any rate, simply wasn't in the air at all. For a moment it seemed so impossibly silly that he actually felt like laughing aloud about it but suddenly he was uneasily struck by the fact that the figure now no longer beating her hands on the taffrail was a pitifully lonely one. In some curious way the very absence of any movement in it gave it a sharp and painful restlessness.

She was staring straight down to the sea, dirty with oil-scum, scraps of paper and strands of packing straw as it flopped between ship and quayside, when he moved a few yards along the deck and said:

'Pardon me, but have you any idea of the name of this place? It looks rather fascinating. I'm not awfully good at names.'

She didn't look at him.

'None whatever.'

'Fascinating I think it looks. Might be a good place to stay. Wouldn't you think so?'

8

'These Greek ports all look the same to me.'

'Oh! do they?'

'I've seen them all. I'm sick to death of them. Still, when you've been travelling for over ten months—'

'Ten months? That's a long time. With the other lady?'

'We travel everywhere together.'

Suddenly the girl put on a pair of dark sun-glasses. Jack Marsden noticed now that her hands were trembling and he stared away at the bicycle lovers, oblivious of all other movement in the white morning sun.

'What was all that talk about war? I was surprised to hear that. That can't be true, can it? I haven't seen a paper for days.'

'It was in the papers yesterday. Kennedy is—'

'You don't really believe war is going to start, do you?'

'Yes, I do. Don't you?'

'Far from it.'

'You're English, aren't you?'

'Yes.'

'I suppose this is that fine old English phlegm coming out?'

Jack Marsden smiled in a teasing sort of way.

'You should really take your sun-glasses off when you say things like that. Otherwise I can't tell if you mean it or not.'

Greatly to his surprise she took them off, nervously dangling them to and fro.

'You've actually got a sense of humour. I didn't think Englishmen ever had.'

'Here and there you'll find one,' he said and smiled again.

She seemed, by this time, to have calmed down a fraction and for the first time she actually lifted her face and looked at the sky, utterly cloudless and already mistily blue with heat, and drew a long deep breath, as if with relief or even pleasure. As she did so, her bust, up-drawn under the turquoise blouse, looked so firm and correct in line and all proportions that he thought, for a moment, that it might not be real. A second later she saw him looking at it and again put on her spectacles.

'I'm sorry you're rushing home. I think this would be a marvellous place to stay.'

'Then why don't you?'

'I might, yet. They'll be at least another hour loading stuff on. They always are.'

She took off her spectacles again, biting tensely at the ends of them. Her mouth, which had seemed rather hard and tight during the exchange about war and cockroaches, now seemed a little softer. But again she saw him looking at her and again put on her spectacles.

'At least we might go ashore and get a cup of coffee,' Jack Marsden said. 'Better than that filthy ship's breakfast. I was nearly sick yesterday.'

'You can say that again. I'm with you there.'

'What about it? I see what looks like a café farther along the quayside.'

She confessed she was dubious. She was scared they might get left behind. And what then?

'We'd spend a nice, quiet, peaceful war together.'

She actually laughed at this and the sound, he thought, was pleasant.

'I could certainly eat some breakfast,' he said. 'I'll go and find out how long we'll be.'

He went away, found a purser and came back with the not unexpected news that the ship would be another hour and a half before departing, perhaps longer.

'What about it?' he said. 'Are you game?'

'I don't see any reason why not.'

'What about the other lady? Ought you to tell her?'

'I don't think so. In her present mood she's thinking more of herself than me.'

Ashore, beyond where the concourse of peasants, cars, donkeys, mules and bicycles thinned out, they sat by a window in a little café with a white tiled floor and a curtain of coloured beads across the entrance. A girl brought coffee and milk, thin slices of bread with green figs, butter and honey.

'My God, this is good. You can taste oil in all the food aboard. I mean engine oil.'

She sipped coffee, her arms crooked on the top of the table. Now and then she took another deep breath and then blew gently on her coffee, trying to cool it down.

'You're unwinding a bit. You were very angry.'

'We have these rows. They've been getting a bit more frequent lately though.'

'Are you great friends? If not the time has obviously come to kiss and part.'

'Not so easy.'

He spread honey thickly on a slice of bread. There was a taste of flowers in it that was like a morning in a summer meadow.

'You had quite a go last night too. She swept out at dinner.'

'Yes. That was why I didn't sleep in the cabin. It wasn't the cockroaches so much.'

'She doesn't look happy.'

'You're very observant, aren't you?'

He said he supposed he was, in a way; but it was really that he was interested in people.

'Is that why you lured me ashore?'

'No: but it's dull travelling if you don't talk to people.'

'And sometimes it's even duller if you do. By the way, where are you going from here?'

'I don't think I am going. I've half made up my mind to stay.'

He spread honey on a second slice of bread and then took a fat dead-ripe green fig and put it on his plate.

'You're not eating anything. This honey is marvellous. Nectar.'

'I just like the coffee. How long would you stay?'

'Until I'm bored. The boats come round every two or three days.'

She seemed to ponder on this, slowly sipping her coffee and now and then blowing on it softly again.

'I wish I had these impulses.'

Laughing quietly, he confessed to being surprised. He thought all women were addicted to impulses.

'The schedule doesn't leave any room for impulses. It's all down in black and white. Arrive Piraeus 18.00 hours, arrive Athens 19.30 hours; 9.00 hours depart for tour of city and the Acropolis. 24.00 hours: see Acropolis by moonlight. Thursday at leisure. Friday—'

While she talked he gazed across the bay. No rain ever seemed to have fallen on the smouldering, fissured mountain slopes that were reflected into the still waters like rocky breasts. A calm as eternal as the hills themselves lay on the curved bright waterfront, where nasturtiums like tangerine trumpets sang from blistered walls. Not a breath of air stirred in the fawn curtain of fish nets hanging above the many blue and white boats drawn up on a scalded strip of shore.

'I think that's why we quarrel so much. We have to put the impulses in. To relieve the tension.'

He didn't say anything in answer to this. The peace of the bay had him locked in a powerful embrace that turned, all of a sudden, into utter captivation.

'I've made up my mind,' he said. 'I'm going to stay.'

'I—'

'Look at that scene. That bay. Look at it. You talk about war. There's eternal peace for you.'

'About to be shattered.'

'All the more reason to enjoy it while we can.'

He discovered suddenly that she had fallen victim to a deep captivation of her own. For the first time she was staring him full in the face, half in a dream.

'You're looking very hard at me. Have I said something I shouldn't?'

'No. No. It was just that—'

'Just what?'

She drank briefly at her coffee, smiled and then put down her cup.

'I just envy you. That's all. I mean that you're free to—'

'Envy me? I thought you wanted to go home?'

It was now her turn not to answer.

'It's all so brilliant and fresh.' Jack Marsden looked again with rising pleasure at the toy blocks of houses, all flat-roofed and vivid as solid cubes of paint in the sun. 'It all looks so new – but of course it does. It's new since the earthquake.'

'Earthquakes? They don't have them here?'

'By God they do. This place was flattened. I remember now.'

Between the scarred ageless hills and the new toy waterfront a boat raised a copper sail without catching the slightest breath of wind.

'If you envy me so much why don't you stay too?'

He was eating a second fig and now he looked up from a short contemplation of its pink heart to see her face pained with incredulous astonishment.

'Me? How on earth could I possibly do that?'

'Simple. Go back to the ship, fetch your bags and set yourself down here. These figs are simply marvellous.'

'But it wouldn't be fair to Beatrice.'

'No?'

'I simply couldn't desert her – just like that.'

He chose a third fig for himself, begging her at

the same time to take one too, but she declined with a short shake of her head, saying:

'We haven't done Venice yet. Nor Spain. We've got two whole months to come in Spain. And then Vienna and Salzburg—'

'At the same time you envy me.'

'Yes, but only in the sense – By the way what are you going to do here?'

He wiped fig juice from his chin, casually.

'Lead the simple life. Forget papers, headlines, scares and all that. Drink a lot of wine. Sleep a lot. Swim a lot. Forget a lot I wish I'd never remembered—'

'But that's almost immoral. It's the worst sort of escaping—'

'Think so? I find it perfect.'

'But with so much going on in the world – I mean this awful threat of war. Don't you really think war is coming?'

'No.'

'Doesn't the mere thought of it scare you?'

'No. After all, there might be another earthquake before I've finished my fig.'

She looked at him with amazed disbelief, lips slightly parted, and he looked straight back at her in return. It was only the second full glance for longer than a moment or two that they had exchanged since leaving the ship and he realised for the first time that she was younger than he had first thought she was. Worry and tension had even marred her good looks. Now, minute by minute, her face was relaxing.

'If you're really staying hadn't you better be going to fetch your baggage?'

'Plenty of time.' He held her again in another full glance, straight in the eyes. Her pupils had many minute streaks of gold in them, rather like the veins you find in certain pebbles. 'What about you fetching yours?'

'First you lure me ashore. Then you lure me to stay.'

'I don't care for this word lure. I think you're scared.'

'Nonsense. I've a schedule to complete with a friend and I'm going to complete it.'

He picked himself a fourth and final fig, putting it to his lips for a caressing second or two without biting the skin. The gesture, almost an act of kissing, was lost on her and he said:

'After all you've got to escape some time.'

'Escape? What on earth from?'

'Oh! nothing. Perhaps I should pay the bill after all and go and get my bag.'

She didn't speak for another minute or two. He did nothing either about fetching his bag and they merely sat quietly. The Greek girl who had served them with breakfast presently came through from the kitchen, walked through the bead curtain and stood idly in the sun outside. She had a dark pretty head and a good strong bosom and bare honey-brown legs and he watched her.

One of the impulses she confessed she never experienced all at once made the American girl say:

'Would you mind awfully if I had some fresh coffee? That's if there's time.'

'Of course not. I'll call the girl.'

He went outside and tapped the girl on the shoulder. She started and gave him a lustrous smile with dark eyes, openly. He smiled back and with his eyes followed the honey-brown legs as she went back into the café.

'I believe I begin to see now why you want to stay on the island.'

'It's as good a reason as any,' he said and he thought her face flushed, but whether from embarrassment or slight vexation it was impossible to tell. 'By the way my name's Jack Marsden. Just in case we might ever meet again.'

'I'm sorry – I should have introduced myself. I'm Ruth Forbes. My companion's name is Beatrice Keller, Mrs Keller.'

'She seems to be rather older than you.'

'Quite a bit.'

'You're very lucky to be able to afford a long trip like this.'

'Lucky? I saved up for three years if you call that lucky. I even went without dinner three times a week. Even then I couldn't have done it if Mrs Keller hadn't helped with the fare. That's another reason why I have to keep this schedule. I've got to get my money's worth. And hers too.'

'Nothing like getting your money's worth,' he said.

The full implication of this remark was lost on her as the Greek girl came back with the coffee. Again he exchanged a smile with her.

'Will you have coffee too?'

'No thanks.' He gave the Greek girl a note for his bill and she went away to the kitchen for change. 'It's getting hot already. It'll be blistering by midday.'

Even as he said this the reposeful surface of the bay leapt up in a million little crests, all like silver horns. The mysterious and sudden breath of wind died as suddenly as it had sprung up and in a second the crests were drowned, the sea as flat as a sheet of tin again.

With her back to the sea she missed this sudden and arresting phenomenon, as beautiful as any-thing he had seen that morning, and he said:

'Ah! you missed that. That was lovely. A sudden breeze sprang up and the bay was full of little waves.'

She turned abruptly to look at the bay. And for some moments, watching her, he was held in a new captivation. The small soft curls of rosy-blonde hair that grew on her neck suddenly roused in him a great impulse to touch her. It was rather like wanting to caress a young and furry creature who hadn't quite grown up.

'Perhaps it'll happen again. But you'll have to look quickly. You have to snatch at these moments.'

Without turning her head she said:

'Well, at any rate you'll have plenty of time to see it again.'

'It would be nice to see it with you.'

The words sprang out from pure impulse. He thought she flushed slightly again, but without turning her head or saying a word in answer.

'I mean it. I'm quite serious. Why don't you stay?'

'It's quite out of the question. It's the most irrational thing I ever heard.'

'Not half as irrational as travelling on that ghastly ship and drooling from place to place all over Europe looking at ruins.'

'You shouldn't say that. You were on the ship yourself.'

'Only because I missed a better one.'

She turned at last from looking across the

bay. By now some tension had returned to her face. The lips had hardened and narrowed again.

'I feel a bit upset,' she said. 'Would you mind if we went back now?'

The Greek girl, a moment or two later, brought his change. Not fully aware of what he was doing he tipped her several more *drachmas* than he need have done and hardly bothered to return her smile.

'If anything I said upset you I'm awfully sorry.'

'Nothing you said.'

They began walking back to the ship. The concourse of donkeys, mules, people and bicycles seemed, he thought, thicker than ever. A jungle of cargo, all bales and boxes, swung about the air.

'It was nothing you said. I suppose I'm just homesick, that's all. The ship got on my nerves.'

He followed her up the gangway and on to the deck of the ship. He looked instinctively for the shape of her legs and was slightly vexed to discover again that she was wearing slacks. Nevertheless the spare good lines of her figure were well revealed and he also once again found himself looking at the nape of her neck and the small rose-blonde nest of hair.

On board, at the head of the mahogany

companion-way, he saw a waiting figure of formidable immobility, its hands still strongly thrust into the pockets of the impossibly wide duck shorts. This, he told himself, must be Mrs Keller and suddenly there was something strangely unpleasant in the air.

# 2

'Where in Heaven's name have you been all this time?'

Mrs Keller's eyes were an oily, slaty brown, like the skin of an eel. Her voice was guttural and drab. There was something Teutonic about the placing of the cheek-bones, which were too high up in the yeasty face, and about the nose, with its too large, squarish nostrils.

'This gentleman simply asked me to go ashore for a cup of coffee, that's all.'

'Gentleman?'

The sneer instantly angered Jack Marsden but he said nothing and managed to keep his temper and turned abruptly to go down the companion-way to his cabin. In his last glimpse of the girl he saw that all the tension had come back to her face. Her lower lip was trembling.

He was hardly out of ear-shot when Mrs Keller said:

'You're not going to tell me this is some sort of pick-up, are you?'

'A friendly cup of coffee hardly constitutes a pick-up.'

'Friendly? Men on board ships are friendly for one reason only. As you well know.'

The girl had nothing to say. Mrs Keller was sweating slightly. Oily beads hung on the small hairs of her upper lip. The possessive, distasteful beat in her voice rose with aggressive sharpness.

'I've told you over and over again how much I hate you going off without word. I've worried my head off. I've searched the entire ship for you. Besides I should have thought you had more pride.'

'My pride is my own affair.'

'Well, as long as you think so.'

'What I think is also my own affair.'

'I don't agree. Not entirely. It concerns me too. Equally. If not more. Who would be to blame if anything happened to you?'

'The coffee was doped, of course.'

'Now it's your turn to be sarcastic. For goodness' sake pull yourself together.' A slight lowering of the tone of Mrs Keller's voice gave it a harsher and more sneering dominance. 'I told you before. You've got war-scare on the brain. You're scared and you get ill-tempered.'

'I'm—'

24

'He's English, isn't he?'

Jack Marsden at this moment was coming back up the steps of the companion-way, carrying his one and only piece of baggage.

'Yes, I'm English. What of it?'

In silence Mrs Keller gave him a glance of flat but all-encompassing contempt. Sweat had run down to the upper edges of her rather orange lipstick, melting it. The effect was to give her entire face a look at once sinister and covetous: almost evil, he thought.

Without a word she turned abruptly at the head of the companion-way and walked out to the upper deck.

After a few moments' silence the girl said, obviously having great difficulty in forming the words:

'I'm sorry about that. Awfully sorry.'

'No need for you to be sorry.'

She brought her hands together in an abrupt, uplifted gesture of protest. He instinctively looked down at them and discovered, for the first time and to his infinite astonishment, that she was wearing a ring on the third finger of her left hand. He simply couldn't think how he had failed to notice the small square topaz before except that the stone was almost exactly the colour of her sun-burnt fingers.

She became aware of his discovery at once and

immediately dropped both hands as if greatly embarrassed about something and then just as quickly raised the right one again and took off her sun-glasses.

'Well, I see you've got your bag. You're really going to stay.'

'It would do you a lot of good to stay too.'

'I can't do that.'

The sun-glasses jigged about in her hands as if electrically charged.

'Well, I don't suppose we shall ever—'

At this moment the purser walked past and Marsden checked him and said:

'Oh! I'm getting off here for a few days. Could you tell me about hotels?'

'But you've got a round ticket, sir.'

'That doesn't matter. Can you tell me about hotels?'

'There's the *Miramar* – that way.' The purser pointed inland, toward a central point of the bay. 'The only other one is the *Helios*.' He pointed in an exactly opposite direction, towards the open sea. 'Outside the town. About a mile. *Helios* is better. Has little bungalows right on the shore. You can dive into the sea from your bed.'

Jack Marsden laughed and thanked him. The *Helios* it would be, he said. And when would the *San Philippa* be back?

'Four days from now, sir.'

Neither the laugh not the last sentences of the conversation had any effect on the girl, who might simply not have been listening. The eyes which were so like little golden pebbles seemed almost sightless. Then suddenly the sun-glasses started jigging again and for a moment he thought she would drop them.

'It's been wonderfully nice meeting you,' he said. 'I shan't forget.'

Again she was at a loss for anything to say. Still the eyes had the strange look of sightlessness which he suddenly tried hard to disperse by joking:

'Think of me sometimes while you're slogging at your cultural ruins, won't you? Wasting away here, the dreadful lotus-eater, doing nothing—'

The joke, though misfiring, had the effect of waking her. The eyes seemed to click. In a moment he could have sworn he detected the smallest touch of moisture on their lower lids and he had sense enough to know that he might well have hurt her.

Before he could say or do anything about this a sudden raucous blast from the ship's siren split the air, making the girl jump as if someone had hit her with a whip. The blast was repeated twice more and she stood all the time with her fore-fingers in her ears, the sun-glasses dangling and jigging, the surface of the topaz flashing on her left hand.

One after the other the siren blasts raced across the bay. Echoes cracked against bare treeless rock and came leaping back like barking animals in pursuit of each other. When it was all over and the air was silent again the girl said:

'I always jump. I'm never ready for it. It always catches me unawares.'

There seemed, he thought, something almost childlike about this remark. He was touched and half-wished, for a second or two, that he wasn't going ashore. Then he remembered the odious orange lips of Mrs Keller and was glad he was going after all.

'Well, I suppose that means me.' He changed his bag from his right hand to his left, ready to shake hands with her. He smiled and she, in turn, smiled faintly in reply. 'Good-bye. I still can't help wishing you were coming with me.'

'Thank you, no. Not this time.'

'There won't be another time.'

'No,' she said, 'I don't suppose there will be, will there? Good-bye. Thanks again for the coffee.'

'Good-bye,' he said again. 'Good-bye.'

The palm of her hand was hot and moist. Something about the touch of her fingers prompted in him a moment of self-reproach and he said:

'I wasn't really very observant, after all, was I? I didn't really see your ring until after I said that about your staying here. I'm very sorry. Otherwise I wouldn't—'

'Oh! that doesn't matter. It really doesn't matter.'

He gave her a final smile and said, suddenly a trifle nervous himself, something about the best of everything. 'Thanks. And to you,' she said and a moment later he turned and walked down the gangway.

His first act, on shore, was to look back. He was pleased to see her standing by the taffrail, sunglasses dangling in her hand, at almost the same place where he had first met her. He smiled and half-waved his hand and she lifted hers in reply. She seemed unexpectedly less tall, he thought, against the old gaunt black structure of the ship but the sun-brown face seemed brighter now.

He watched the gangway being hauled up and the ropes being cast away. In another minute or two the *San Philippa* began to move from the quay. And then once again, sudden and raucous, the siren blew another blast.

The girl, with a little cry, automatically lifted her fingers to her ears. The sun-glasses went spinning from her hands, fell like a pair of pupilless eyes to the water, actually floated there for a second or two and then sank.

He waited for the siren to die; and then, funnelling his hands, called up to her:

'Now you really will have to come back. I'll dive for them tomorrow. You really will.'

And in that moment, as she finally waved her hand, he saw that she was actually laughing.

# 3

The hotel turned out to be not one but four miles along the coast road and he drove there in an ancient saloon taxi with fawn curtains at the windows and two holes in the floor.

The road went like a white switch-back between little valleys where bamboo grew thick and already papery dry in dykes and precipitous yellow cliffs of rock that seemed to glower, cracked and roasted, in the great glare of sun. In the valleys there were also many little orchards of lemon and orange and a few of peach and almond. Old walls of stone, crumbling away, disappeared into intense entanglements of bushes and vine, crowned everywhere by pink and sometimes creamy oleander trees. In the heat of morning very little moved: a woman drawing water from a stand-pipe and carrying it away in a rose-brown pitcher on her head, a few scrawny sheep panting in the shade of trees, a goat trailing black droppings in the

white dust of the road, an incredibly small
donkey bearing a shrouded woman up a path,
scattering a red hen and her brood of yellow
chicks. A bird of hawk-like appearance, planing
silently, cast its shadow on a sea that had no other
blemish on its blue-white face and once a rock
slid down from a rain-scarred cliff, dustily
carving a little path through low clumps of
myrtle before disappearing altogether. And then
the hotel: white and new, its separate bungalows
of bamboo set out among crippled olive trees of
prodigious age on the curving fringe of a little
bay.

The unperturbed tranquillity of it all spread
through him like a drug. For the next two days
he swam frequently, drank a good deal of resinous
red wine, slept a lot and walked a little, floating
in a vacuum. In the torrid, arid heat he even
lacked, at first, the will to be bored.

Every day, immediately after sunrise, the great
chorus of cicadas began. His bungalow of bamboo
and thatch, sitting under the black shade of an
olive tree of enormous spread and great age, its
tortuous branches like the limbs of a giant black
wrestler, was the centre of countless singing
whirlwinds. In some way, as he grew used to them,
they created their own peculiar hush: an im-
penetrable and perpetual barrier of sound more
silent than silence itself and as ageless and

indestructible as the tiers of mountains across the bay.

About nine o'clock, by which time the heat was already putting scorching daggers down through every leaf-gap in the olive tree, a young Greek waiter, dressed in white shirt, royal blue trousers and a broad scarlet waist sash, brought his breakfast, setting it down on the bungalow verandah with many smiles. The fresh bread, the butter, the honey, the coffee and the fruit – once there were figs again and on the second morning mulberries and peaches – were all as he wished them and he ate and drank within twenty yards of a sea that had no vestige of disturbance on its pale grey-blue surface and hardly a wave on the fringe of it big enough to break on the white-hot shore.

Apart from the waiter there was no other living creature to bother him except a pair of house-martins who had built a nest under the crutch of a post at the end of the verandah and a grey wagtail, delicately arrowed with lemon on breast and wings, that darted and ran and picked at flies hanging above scorched strings of sea-weed along the beach. Nervously the martins hung on the air, frightened at the flash of a spoon or the lifting of a coffee cup, waiting to enter the nest. With equally nervous delicacy the wagtail pranced every now and then into air, as if its

B

little spider feet had been scalded by the great heat of the sand.

At mid-morning he swam for half an hour. The water was warm and milky. A few small fish, alabaster in colour and half transparent, swam in lazy shoals close to the white sea-bed. Sometimes a boat passed, not using a sail because of the extreme stillness of the day, its engine duttering monotonously. Once or twice, farther away, looking no larger than a centipede under the great line of mountains, a ship passed, soundless, creeping southward.

After his swim he lay in the shade of the big olive, almost embalmed in the great murmurous song of cicadas, and turned over in his mind thoughts of Ruth Forbes. He saw the nape of her neck again, the sun-brown skin and the nest of rose-blonde hair. He thought a good deal about the ring on her finger and wondered what sort of man had put it there.

The uselessness of all this did nothing to deter him from reasoning that the more he thought of the ring the less sense it made. Whichever way he looked at it he thought the ring seemed odd. A pretty patient fellow must be waiting somewhere, he thought, while the two women made their tedious pilgrimage of the world. A year of separation would surely try the best of men.

Several times he cursed himself for not having

taken her address and once he started a mental chase of her half across Europe, searching for her in Venice, Vienna, Rome and Spain. Again the uselessness of all this did nothing to deter him. Sometimes in the great hush made by the cicadas he fancied he could hear her voice. It was a very pleasant voice, its accent slightly southern, with a gentle uplift of enquiry at the end of its sentences.

Once he talked aloud to it and said:

'I was an idiotic fool not to come on the ship with you, wasn't I? Why didn't you ask me if I would? I suppose you were too shy to ask me.'

Into these imaginary exchanges the voice of Mrs Keller, almost animal-like in its lack of all refinement, obtruded like a preying snarl. He saw again the odious orange lips, the sweat beads on the upper lip and the eyes of eel-like oiliness that had in them far more than a glint of mere possessiveness. They too, like the voice, seemed to belong to an animal bent on prey.

Aloud he spoke to Mrs Keller too:

'You're the sort of woman it would be a pleasure to hate. In fact I hate you now. No, I'm glad I didn't stay on the boat. Heaven knows what I might have done to you.'

The afternoons were lost in sleep. At night a moon like a great golden balloon lifted itself from behind the mountains that by this time had taken on the look of sleeping dinosaurs. As it rose and

paled, flooding the sea-face with a vast path of
light, somewhere between phosphorescence and
silver, his thoughts turned to Ruth Forbes again
and once more he talked to her:

'God, why aren't you here? Why couldn't you
have done something irrational for once in your
life? Something on impulse. Why couldn't you
have put an end to your culture crawling and
given your feminine impulses a chance for once?
God, why couldn't you have come? Why couldn't
you?'

On the second night, when he turned into the
bungalow towards midnight, he had worked
himself into such a state of restlessness, fed by the
glare of moonlight, that he found sleep quite impossible.

He lay for more than an hour on his back,
staring upward, hands clasped behind his head,
thinking, imagining things, damning and hating
Mrs Keller and talking once again to Ruth
Forbes:

'You could have been here with me. Just the
two of us. We could have swum by moonlight. I
could have given you all the pleasure a girl could
want. All the pleasure in the world. Oh! I
suppose it wasn't to be. I suppose it just wasn't in
the lap of the gods. Oh! damn the gods. Blast
them—'

He suddenly got up, put on a pair of slippers

and walked in his pyjamas along the shore. The moon was full overhead by now; the great path of light had expanded to a vast shimmering circle. A breath as of floating honey, the fragrance from some invisible nocturnal-scented tree, filled the air, taunting all his senses.

In a mixture of impatience and then hostility against something, he didn't know quite what, he started to pick up pebbles and hurl them at the phosphorescent face of the sea.

Then he knew quite well, at last, that he was bored.

# 4

In the morning he was woken by several fretting toots of a ship's siren across the bay. Half hoping and half expecting to see the *San Philippa* coming back, he got out of bed, put on a pair of slippers and went and stood on the shore.

A small ship, all white except for a broad band of chicory blue across her one funnel, was creeping in at half speed under the walls of mountain. He watched her idly for a few minutes and then decided that here, at any rate, was one way of killing boredom. He would go down to the port and watch her moor and unload her passengers. It would do something to while another morning away.

Half an hour later he was lucky enough to be offered a lift in a fruit and vegetable truck delivering goods at the hotel. The driver and his wife sat in the cab, leaving room for one other person, but at the last moment a young waiter came running out of the hotel, begging a lift too, and finally he and Jack Marsden sat in the back of the truck, legs dangling out from behind.

The waiter, who spoke English, was thin, sad-faced and very talkative. With enthusiasm he described many points of the passing landscape. 'Up there, sir, is a monastery. You will see it when we are round the next bend. And over there, sir, on the point, that's a little palace. Sometimes the King will stay there.'

And what was that little town across the bay? Jack Marsden wanted to know. He saw its lights at night.

'It's a little town called Stephanos, sir. From there you can get a bus to Athens. Sometimes it's quicker than waiting for the big boats, sir.'

And how did one get across there? Swim?

'Oh! no sir. Demetrius and his brother have a little cabin cruiser. They go across sometimes to see their sisters. They take people for trips around the island too. You'll see them come past the hotel in the boat, sir. You might like to take a trip sometime.'

I might at that, he thought.

A few minutes later he was at the port: watching, with amazed bemusement, a female Greek guide marshalling, like a podgy and peremptory sergeant-major, a company of twenty-odd tourists down the ship's gangway. A small reckless-looking bus without windows stood waiting on the quayside and towards this, incredibly prompted by occasional snipping blasts on a football whistle, the Greek guide marshalled her company. Cameras slung about their necks, guide-books held like bibles, a filmy patience in every eye, the company stood almost to attention, meekly awaiting orders for the day.

'Are we all here? Is everybody with us?'

The guide actually counted heads. Her voice had the charm of a big, cracked bell. Her black hair, dry and stiff, was like that of a golliwog and protruded flatly outwards from under the brim of what seemed to be a large white night cap.

'I forget how many of you speak English. How many speak English?'

Two timid hands were raised from somewhere in the centre of the waiting ranks.

'Two only. That being so I shall speak only in French and German. It is otherwise too exhausting. Do you speak either French or German, you English pair?'

'No.'

'It is all very unfortunate. Very well, I shall try my best.' She blew vehemently on the whistle. 'Everybody into the bus. There is no time to spare.'

The cracked bell repeated its orders in three languages. The company filed into the bus, its heads actually counted again, as if by some chance one might already have deserted.

To Jack Marsden's astonishment he suddenly found that the guide was on the point of counting him too.

'Are you with us?' she said in German. 'I can't remember whether you are with us.'

'I'm afraid not.'

'Ah! you are English. You are not with us? I see. Would you care to come with us? You may do so if you wish.'

'Where are you going?'

'It is a conducted tour of the island. We shall see the monastic ruins and the Sacred Lake. We shall also see the Archaic Temple—'

He recalled his reproaches to Ruth Forbes about her culture crawling pilgrimage of the world but at the same time, struck again by the thought of another long boring day, incredibly found himself saying:

'All right. Thank you very much. I'll come.'

'One hundred and twenty drachmas, please.'

He paid his money and got into the bus, which presently shook to life like a hard-worked threshing engine and took off inland, fiercely. On the very instant of departure the voice of the guide threw its brassy babble, in three languages, into a microphone, from whence it poured crackling vomit through a loud-speaker.

'Will the English pay good attention please? I am speaking in English now. Below, to your left, you observe the ruins of an ancient fort. This fort, first constructed in—'

He sat on the back seat of the bus, alone, only half listening. Staring out, he saw the road begin to rise steeply from the sea. The coastal strip of vegetation, rich with its oleanders, mulberries, olives, vines, acacias, trumpeting nasturtiums and prickly pears, dropped gradually away. A brownish-ochre rock, bitterly dry, took its place, the long grasses among it lifeless, scalded to the colour of straw.

'Attention, I am speaking now in English again—'

The deep clefts of dusty rock resolved themselves, after half an hour, into a plateau where great panels of stone lay everywhere like fallen grave-stones. Time had scorched hieroglyphic epitaphs into the surface of them in deep scribbled veins. Only straw-coloured grass grew among them and numbers of flat-flowered thistles, yellowish too, that might have been cut from steel.

The bus stopped suddenly, the whistle blew and Jack Marsden, getting out at his leisure, well behind the ordered company, discovered that here must be the Archaic Temple. A strongish wind had sprung up by now and was whistling

43

with unexpected treachery, hot and fierce, across the grave-stones. No more than half a dozen ruined marble columns remained in the centre of the plateau, far below which the sea was a deep ultramarine strip, absolutely still and shining in the sun.

He walked towards the ruins, still well behind the company. Cameras clicked and whirred. A more savage gust of wind than usual set every blade of grass quivering as from a vast electric shock and a man's cream panama hat bowled and bounced across the rocks, its owner in dishevelled pursuit, the company laughing.

'Here we see the central court. Observe here the Doric peristyle and also the Doric porticos. This establishment was—'

Jack Marsden sat down on a rock, twenty yards from where the guide was speaking in German now. A woman's voice in English said:

'You're rather like my husband. You don't seem to be very interested. I believe he actually let his hat blow away on purpose.'

He stood up, to find himself talking to a woman of sixty or so, ordinary enough, carrying a cream sunshade.

'I'm afraid I'm not. I find something cold and cruel about these temples.'

'Really? I wonder why that should be?'

'The columns all look somehow callous to me.'

'You mean you find none of them at all beautiful?'

'I can't say I do.'

'I must say I find them extraordinarily beautiful.'

'Give me a tree with a few flowers on it or some fruit and you can talk about beauty. But not that callous-looking stone, not that stuff. It's like a graveyard up here.'

'But the spirit of it. The antiquity. The history—'

'History,' he said. 'What's history?'

She seemed bewildered by this sudden and unexpected show of rudeness and half turned away. In turn he was acutely aware of having, for a second or two, behaved badly and in a far kindlier voice said:

'Oh! by the way, can you tell me – where does your ship carry on to from here?'

'Back to Piraeus.'

'Oh! yes. This afternoon?'

'Yes. I think at five o'clock.'

'I see. Do you think there might be some chance of a passage?'

'I'm sure of it. There's hardly anyone aboard.'

He thanked her and walked suddenly away. A strong and curious premonition, not merely an impulse, all at once told him to walk back to the hotel and get ready to leave. Perhaps boredom itself had set off the sudden change in his mind; but without waiting to ponder or consider it he was suddenly leaping quickly across the plateau of stones, his back turned on the temple.

A shrill blast of the whistle split the air. Dismay gave to the voice of the Greek guide an ever shriller brassiness as she called:

'Attention, Mr English! Where are you going? I am about to explicate the temple in English. Do you not want to see the Sacred Lake? We leave in fifteen minutes now.'

'No lake is sacred,' he said to himself and without pausing or answering went on.

He walked down the long precipitous mountain road to the town, meeting in the hot gully between the rocks only an occasional figure on a donkey, a woman carrying a tin water-can on her head and a few scabby goats feeding, together with stray chickens, under olive and acacia trees. Although it was still not far beyond mid-morning the grip of heat was almost savage, torturing his eyes. The dust of the road broke under his feet into smoky fires and every sign of early freshness had gone from the air.

At the outskirts of the town he stopped at a café, bought himself a large bottle of mineral water, drank half of it standing in the street outside and then poured the rest over his hair and face and shoulders. He had been walking for an hour and a half and he longed, more than anything, to get to the sea.

He got to the sea, by the bungalows of the hotel, about twelve o'clock. No lake, however sacred, could have looked more inviting than the tranquil, sparkling bay and he was already stripping off his shirt as he walked along the shore.

'Sir! Mr Marsden, sir. Sir! Mr Marsden.'

At the sound of the voice he turned and saw a young Greek waiter, in white shirt, blue trousers and scarlet sash, hurrying after him with what seemed to be a letter in his hand.

It was in fact a telegram. 'Arriving Thursday by *San Philippa*,' it read. 'Would so much like to talk. Forbes.'

# 5

The curious thing was that she didn't talk: at least not very much, in the beginning.

The first significant thing that struck him about her arrival was that she was no longer wearing slacks. Instead she had on a light, pretty tangerine-coloured dress and, what he thought to be still more significant, a pair of white lace gloves, which she kept drawing a little more tightly over her hands as she walked slowly down the gangway of the ship.

'Well, here I am,' she said and her voice was strangely distant, almost unreal.

She gave him the faintest of nervous smiles and they got into the ancient curtained taxi he had hired before. At first it struck him that the presence of the driver might have something to do with her silence, but even when he himself talked she hardly answered. He wasn't to know until some long time afterwards that it was really the acutest embarrassment, something very like shame, that kept her so quiet that morning. On the ship she had reproached herself bitterly, a dozen times, for having sent the telegram at all and now she was desperately afraid that because of it he would think her cheap. Even if she could have explained at that time why she had sent the telegram it wouldn't have helped very much. The fact was it was all done now and she only hoped that in time she would be able to give it all a rational explanation.

'I think you'll like the hotel. It's on this principle of having a central building where you have your meals and so on and then you have small bungalows along the beach. I got them to reserve the one next to mine for you. There aren't more than a dozen people here.'

She uttered a barely audible 'I see,' and he went on:

'The swimming's terrific. I expect you'd like a swim?'

'Not today.'

At the hotel a boy put her bags into the bungalow while she stood outside, nervously fingering her gloves, almost as if waiting for Jack Marsden to go.

'I expect you'd like a drink?' he said.

'Thank you, yes. I would.'

'They have a light white wine, local I think. It's pretty good, cold. Would that do?'

'Thank you, yes.'

'I expect you'll want to freshen up a bit. Shall we say in half an hour?'

'No: I'm all right. Have the wine now if you'd like to.'

He told the boy to bring the wine. They sat down in cane chairs, on the verandah, facing the sea. Far out a ship crawled southward, white, centipede-like, much like something in a dream. Backwards and forwards in front of his own verandah the house-martins clung nervously at air and then, with lightning swoops, darted into the nest.

'My friends the martins,' he said. 'I've really got very fond of them. There's a pair of wagtails too. Awfully pretty. I don't know about you, but I'm fond of birds.'

As if this remark wasn't worth any observation she simply sat staring at her gloves, her hands motionless in her lap.

'By the way, it's a good thing you telegraphed. I was all set to leave yesterday afternoon.'

'Why?'

'Bored. Restless. It's absolute perfection here – you couldn't wish for anything better – but you can get bored even with perfection. Funny, I thought a lot about you yesterday. I sometimes think I've got a telepathic sort of mind.'

Again she had no sort of comment to make and presently he said:

'I even took a leaf out of your book and went ruin-crawling. It was like being drilled and marched by a yapping little sergeant-major.'

It wasn't until the boy brought the wine that she spoke again and began to take off her gloves. Even then he was so preoccupied with watching the boy pour out the wine and put the bottle back into the ice-bucket that it was fully three or four minutes before he noticed the gloves lying on the table. When he finally did so he thought he knew the reason for them too.

The topaz ring was no longer on her finger.

The discovery gave him a strange start of excitement. It was exactly as if she had said something extraordinarily intimate to him, perhaps even secretive. He felt completely at a loss for anything to say and for another minute or two simply sat sipping wine, all his senses tuned up and expectant.

At last he asked her if she liked the wine. Yes, she said, and still distantly, she liked it very much. It was wonderfully refreshing.

'Better than some I had on the *San Philippa*. Served at room temperature. Boiling point.'

Though there was a lack of tension in her face,

she seemed preoccupied, he thought, almost to a point of physical weariness. It occurred to him that this might be the cause of all her silences and he said:

'Was the trip exhausting? How far did you go?'

'Brindisi.'

He was on the point of asking her what exactly had suddenly made her come back when he abruptly decided not to. A second later, as if she had actually sensed what he was going to ask, she started to say:

'Well, actually—'

He waited for the rest of the sentence but she didn't go on. It was rather like that nervous clinging to air of one of the house-martins and suddenly, for no sane reason at all, he got the uncanny idea that she was on the verge of telling him some gigantic lie. For some time he couldn't get this preposterous notion out of his head or even find any sort of rational reason for thinking of it.

And then, again as if knowing exactly what he was thinking, she suddenly said:

'I suppose you'll think I'm an awful liar, but I really wasn't coming back. I tried to call you twice on the phone but they told me they couldn't find you. Anyway that's how I knew you were here and why I wired.'

The confessional nature of this speech, even

though it was still flat and distantly delivered, startled and disturbed him. He got the uneasy impression that there was something desperate behind it all: some threat or trouble, even something sinister. Having accused her in his own mind of lacking impulses he now started to feel that whatever impulse had driven her back might well be one of actual despair, possibly even tragic. And then, even as he sat pondering about it, she suddenly changed the subject:

'Aren't you swimming either?' she said.

'Not if you won't. I imagine you must be tired?'

'Not exactly.'

There was something oddly enigmatical about this that disturbed him too. He poured out more wine, filling up the two glasses. In the heat of high morning the ice was already melting to mere globular fragments in the bucket but the bottle was still cold to the touch.

'I expect you'll feel better after a meal and some sleep,' he said. 'You'll find the food a bit of an advance on the *Philippa*.'

'That wouldn't be hard.'

It was the one and only remark she had made that was in any sense light and free. All the rest had seemed to be, as it were, delivered from a straitjacket. She actually smiled and Jack Marsden, feeling a sudden communicating sense of relief, laughed briefly in return and said:

'The hotel has an old Ford coupé that one can hire. I don't know how long you're going to stay but I thought we might go over and see a bit of the other side of the island. They get more rain there, I believe. The countryside's more fertile. Not so dried up.'

'It depends how long you'll put up with me.'

He felt an unbearable sadness in this remark; the impulse to get up and touch her in some way, merely perhaps by putting his hand on her arm or shoulder, was almost irresistible, but before he could do or say anything she said:

'Perhaps you'll get bored again and want to go.'

'Oh! Good God, no. That would be—'

'Let's talk about it later, shall we?'

Nothing more was said, either before or during lunch, about the things that seemed to be troubling her. Nor was it time, he thought, to talk about the ring. With food, more wine and then coffee she relaxed a little more and then actually confessed, at the very end of lunch, that she was very tired.

'I'll sleep,' she said. 'I'm really weary.'

He slept too, to be woken about five o'clock by one of the waiters tapping gently on his door.

'There is a telephone call for Miss Forbes,' he said. 'But I can't seem to wake her.'

'Miss Forbes is terribly tired,' he said. 'I'll come along myself and see if it's important. It's probably the shipping agency. She said something about their having her passport.'

He went down, in the scorching afternoon heat, to the main building of the hotel. In a telephone booth he picked up a receiver and said 'Hullo?' and a voice answered:

'Hullo? Who is that? I want to speak to Miss Forbes.'

There was no mistaking the odious, drab, guttural tones of Mrs Keller and he felt all his latent hatred of her streaming furiously back.

'Hullo? Who are you? I want to speak with Miss Forbes.'

'I'm afraid you're mistaken,' he said. 'There's no Miss Forbes here.'

'Who are you? You sound English to me. Are you—'

'Miss Forbes is not here. I'm sorry—'

'You sound to me like the man she met on the boat.'

'Yes: it's me. Marsden.'

'Where's Miss Forbes? Tell me, where's Ruth?'

'How the hell should I know?' he shouted.

'She telegraphed you, didn't she?' the voice was more odiously, more repugnantly guttural now. 'I have information that she telegraphed you.'

'She did nothing of the kind,' he shouted. 'She did not telegraph me and she's not here. Moreover it's bloody hot and I'm catching the boat to Rhodes in half an hour. Good-bye!'

He slammed down the receiver with a final shout and, trembling with anger, nerves dancing, sweat pouring in an almost painful prickling from all over his body, went back to the bungalow. There he stripped, put on his swimming trunks and in a dozen strides was in the sea.

He had again a strong and distasteful impression of having been in the presence of something not merely odious but malevolent, even evil. Even over the long distance wires of the telephone the disembodied voice of Mrs Keller had an unclean and vulturous insistence that chilled and sickened him physically. His blood felt dirty. In revulsion and still in anger he lashed about for several minutes in the sea, wallowing and flopping about like a furious animal on the verge of drowning, now and then actually barking out a few un-intelligible syllables of sheer fury, spitting water, too beside himself to swim.

When he had finally recovered enough to stand up and look about him it was to see Ruth Forbes, in a two-piece swim-suit of pale lemon, standing on the path between the bungalows and the shore.

'I fancied I heard someone tapping on my door a while ago,' she said. 'Was it you?'

57

'No. It wasn't me. No one's been this way.'

'I could have sworn—'

'Oh! you were dreaming,' he said. 'Come in!'

She came down to the sea. She looked astonishingly refreshed and calmed and somehow it was very much as if he were seeing her, he thought, for the first time.

# 6

She enjoyed her first swim so much that, some hours after dinner, she suggested another.

Again the fragrance of some invisible nocturnal flowering tree was heavy all along the shore. The air, utterly without wind, was as soft as silk and the moon again rose like a gigantic balloon from behind the dark line of dinosaurish mountains.

In such circumstances he knew that he ought to have been perfectly happy; but all the time he was aware of being increasingly perplexed and troubled. It was not simply that the odious and sinister nature of Mrs Keller's voice over the telephone still lingered obnoxiously with him; nor was it altogether that he suspected that the girl had been driven by something very exceptional, perhaps fright, to come back to him. It was the queer and uneasy feeling that Mrs Keller herself might be coming back too.

As they sat on the shore, waiting to swim and

watching the path of moonlight broadening on the face of the sea, he suddenly asked her if she knew of a place called Kastoria. He had heard it was a very fine place to go.

'We were going there but the schedule got too tight and we couldn't fit it in. What made you ask?'

'I wondered if you'd like to go there.'

'Why?'

'I simply wondered. It would make a change.'

'But I've only just got here. Besides, I like it here. Don't you?'

'I like it better now you're here.'

Immediately after he had said this she lapsed into one of her long silences. She simply sat staring at the sea: her thoughts, if she had any, far away. Once or twice he tried to start the conversation again but his words hadn't the slightest visible effect on her.

She behaved like this for perhaps another quarter of an hour; then with an abruptness that was almost accusatory she said:

'I suppose you must have thought it terribly odd that I came back here?'

'I knew you must have had a very good reason.'

'Only that?'

'I'm not asking you to tell me if you don't want to.'

Once again she said something strange and enigmatic.

'If I told you it might make it seem odder than ever.'

After that she was quiet again; she seemed to drift away. This time he made no point of starting the conversation again, but presently she caught sight of a shell glittering in the brilliant moonlight on the beach and she leaned over to her left hand to pick it up. The full turn of her body brought the back of her head, with its fascinating nest of light rose-blonde hair, full into view. She played for a few seconds longer with the shell and then before she could turn again he started tenderly stroking the nape of her neck, saying at the same time:

'It wasn't by any chance because you liked me, was it?'

She didn't answer. She still kept her head averted. Then suddenly, still stroking her neck with one hand, he turned her face fully round with the other and pressed his mouth forward to kiss her.

His lips had hardly reached her face when she leapt sharply to her feet. With her face in her hands and her back turned she stood some yards away in the preposterous attitude of an old-fashioned schoolgirl whose shyness had been immensely and profoundly shocked.

He simply couldn't believe it. He got up, walked slowly over to her and said:

'My goodness, whatever's the matter?'

'Don't do that.'

'What else do you expect me to do? I like you. It's a brilliant warm night – I should have thought the occasion was a perfectly idyllic one.'

'I don't care for idyllics.'

'Oh! my God, this is plain silly.'

'To you, perhaps. But not to me.'

She spoke almost as if horrified by this simple and harmless incident and he once again detected in her voice all the brittle tension he had first noticed in her quarrel with Mrs Keller.

'Oh! for Jesus' sake tell me what it's all about,' he said. 'Tell me what's the matter.'

'That's just it. I can't. At least not yet. And trying to kiss me won't help things either.'

For the first time he felt in danger of losing his temper. It was the very last thing he wanted to do and in order to try to avoid it he walked slowly away and stood on the edge of the sea. After some moments of standing there, in which she didn't move either, he said, half to himself:

'I once knew a girl who became paralysed through being jilted. Then she fell in love again and picked up her bed and walked.'

After he had said this she walked slowly over towards him and stood a yard or two away. In the full moonlight, in the very pale lemon two-piece swim-suit, the full front of her figure looked almost entirely naked. The only shadows were those under her breasts, her chin and the inner flanks of her legs. In the naked centre of it all her navel looked like a small and delicate shell itself and as he stared fully at it he started to feel a powerful and intolerable desire to make love to her. She chilled it at once by saying in a flat, cool voice:

'I didn't catch what you said.'

In deliberately level tones he repeated the two sentences and she said:

'Well? Is that supposed to have something to do with me?'

'You're not wearing your ring, are you?'

'If you mean the topaz one that was not an engagement ring.'

'I'm profoundly glad to hear it.'

'If that remark was meant to be ironical I can't say I care for it.'

The situation suddenly seemed to him so impossibly idiotic that he again felt in danger of losing his temper. For a second time he just managed to control it, this time by walking over to her and holding her by the shoulders. As he touched her she stiffened perceptibly and then simply stood staring at him, rigid as a post.

'You're asking an awful lot of me,' he said. 'You come here of your own volition. You swim with me. You stand there half-naked – looking like –

like some damned Greek goddess just risen from the sea in one of those myths of theirs – what the hell do you expect me to do about it? What the hell did you come back here for if you're going to behave like an overwrought schoolgirl?'

'I came back because I thought you were an awfully understanding person. I'll explain it all in time. You can't understand everything all at once, in a moment.'

'Oh! God, I'm sorry,' he said. 'That was pretty boorish of me.'

To his complete astonishment she actually laughed.

'What's so funny?' he said.

'You sounded the real true Englishman just then,' she said and to his still further astonishment suddenly linked one of her arms in his. 'Come on. Let's walk. It'll cool our tempers.'

For another half an hour, arm in arm, they walked along the shore. He cooled easily and was no longer troubled because she didn't talk very much. The sea, locked by dark mountains, illuminated by white fire, shimmering away for mile after mile seemed, the more he looked at it, to have a sense of great mystery about it. The pristine nocturnal beauty of it was as old as eternity and he and Ruth Forbes, he began to feel, were old too, figures out of a long-hidden legend.

'I'm going to ask you one of those damn-fool

hackneyed questions,' he said as they turned to walk back. 'Do you believe there's a pattern? – you know, in all this?'

'Very much.'

'I'm beginning to think so myself,' he said. 'Do you remember I told you how I missed a boat?'

'I remember.'

'I missed it because I got drunk on too much *ouzo* the night before and overslept about three hours. I was going to Rhodes. I wasn't coming here at all.'

'Disgusting man, getting drunk.'

'I warn you that I shall get frequently and disgustingly drunk again if you don't allow me to kiss you within the next seven days.'

'So you're an alcoholic, now, are you?'

'Terrible. I beat women. I have *delirium tremens* at breakfast.'

'How very interesting.'

'I wash in raw whisky.'

'And what do you shave in?'

'Mostly gin. It burns the roots of the beard out.'

'So that's why you look so clean and healthy. I know now.'

By the time they got back to the bungalows she had fully caught his mood and was laughing freely and even gaily now.

'Sleep well,' he said as they stopped to say good night. 'Shall we hire the old car tomorrow?

c

We could take a picnic over to the other side of the island. Would you like that?'

'I should like it very much.'

'Good. We'll do that.'

'Good-night,' she said. 'Sleep well.'

With a final touch of banter he shook her by the hand.

'You don't mind, Miss Forbes, if I shake you by the hand? Unless of course you'd rather I gave you the farewell virginal kiss of a total stranger?'

'As a great concession you may give me the farewell virginal kiss of a total stranger.'

'Good. Thank you. On the forehead of course.'

He kissed her lightly on the centre of the forehead.

'You may also call me Ruth,' she said.

'I am blessed by the gods!' he said. 'I am heady with wine!—'

'Be quiet,' she said, laughing again. 'Go to bed now before you wake the neighbours.'

He went to bed and, drugged by much sea air and no longer troubled by any thought of even the ominous Mrs Keller, slept like a child.

# 7

In the morning all his forebodings were back, darker than ever.

As he drove along the coast road in the old Ford coupé he had hired from the hotel the girl said:

'Oh! by the way, the reception clerk said there had been a telephone call for me yesterday afternoon and that you took it. You didn't tell me.'

'You were fast asleep. It was just the shipping agency checking to see if you had your passport.'

'Why should they do that?'

'Search me. They're not very bright, these people.'

He drove some distance, now uphill, between plantations of young eucalyptus trees, the bare orange-brown earth underneath them heavily scarred by flood veins, before she said:

'He also said the night porter had told him

there had been another in the night. About three o'clock, he thought.'

'Did he say who it was?'

'No. The night porter had gone off duty.'

'Couldn't have been for you. Nobody knows you're here. They really do get their lines crossed in this country.'

At the time she said no more about it; but he was oppressed and uneasy by the thought that she wasn't satisfied.

The road climbed presently into rockier country, thicker than ever with entanglements of neglected vine, bougainvillea falling from decaying walls, mulberries gone wild and always the great blossoming bushes of oleander, some pink, some cream, raising their heads almost as high as the lowest of the cypresses.

When the road fell again, precipitously, it was into a little bay of remarkably limpid water, a shore of dark rocks and a blue and rose-brown village where fishing boats were drawn up to the quayside, and even on it, like squat wide cradles. Fishing nets the colour of rice straw were hanging out to dry or for mending, a few women stitching away at them, gossiping. Every boat had its lantern fixed astern. In the shade of stone arcades glowing with many azure trumpets of morning glory a few fishermen sat drinking, playing with dice or reading papers. Heat shimmered incessantly on the blue skin of water, where a solitary figure, fifty yards out, stood up to his knees, fishing with a line.

Jack Marsden drove the car along the quayside and beyond the harbour. The two of them hadn't spoken much for a quarter of an hour or so, except that he once asked her if she wouldn't like to stop and walk along the quay among the boats and she said simply 'Not now. Perhaps when we come back,' but suddenly with a sharp cry he stopped the car, begging her to look at the sea.

With delight he pointed out to her the sudden little phenomenon of the sea breaking out of its silken calmness into a silvered flurry that might have been a chorus of flying seahorns. This time, quicker than when he had noticed it at their first meeting, she was able to catch the full sight of it at once and sat breathlessly watching it, gold-brown eyes shining, until it died suddenly away, every sparkle of silver instantaneously evaporated.

'Wasn't that marvellous?' he said.

'That's one of the extraordinary things about you,' she said. 'You notice these little incidents so quickly.'

It was far too hot to think of picnicking on the shore and he felt they were very lucky to find a level space of ground, twenty or thirty feet above the sand, shaded by pines. Huge brown walls of rock, fissured deeply and locked together here and there by ancient trees and their naked roots, pine and olive mostly, rose behind them and he thought he could hear from somewhere the falling water of a little stream.

He went to find it and wash his hands. When he came back she had the picnic already opened out and was buttering big chunks of bread and covering them with lapping ears of ham. He uncorked one of the two bottles of wine they had brought with them and poured it out, pale vermilion, into beakers. She was wearing a pair of pale blue linen shorts and a simple cream-coloured blouse and a blue neckerchief to shield her neck from the sun and he sat sipping wine and watching her while she sorted out the rest of the food, cheese, cucumbers, figs, apples and peaches.

Something about the pale blue and cream of her clothes and the domestic nature of the scene gave her an air of sheer repose that for a few minutes suppressed the last of his forebodings. Then just as he was congratulating himself that she herself hadn't perhaps been uneasy after all she looked down at the sea and said:

'You don't think that might have been Beatrice telephoning in the night, do you?'

'Good God, no.'

'It would be like her.'

'She doesn't even know you're here. You didn't tell her, did you?'

'No, I didn't. But you don't know Beatrice. She has uncanny ways of finding out things.'

'Perhaps I would if you'd tell me a little more about her.'

She sipped at the beaker of wine, lost in thought. Here, as everywhere else, the great chorus of cicadas created its own peculiar hush, in some way deeper than silence itself, embalming all the smouldering central core of the day. He was never really aware of listening to it and the silence seemed even more profound than usual as he watched her sipping wine and waited for her to speak again.

'I've wanted to tell you all along, but it isn't easy. Can you bear to listen while you're eating? It's simply that I feel like telling you now.'

'Whichever way you like,' he said.

When she was twenty she worked in the millinery section of a big departmental store and lived in one room and a kitchenette on the edge of Baltimore. Her father was dead and her mother had married pretty quickly again. In this sort of situation it wasn't surprising that she was hungry for companionship or, because she was an over-shy, over-sensitive sort of girl, that she found it difficult to get. She was naturally hungry for love too and she found that even more elusive. Then she suddenly fell like a meteor – the words were her own – for a man named Shaw, a car salesman who got into casual conversation with her at a lunch counter one day.

'Yes, I fell all right. Like a meteor. You could have buried a bus in the hole I made. You know how it is when you fall like that – everybody else thinks you're cooked crazy and you are and it doesn't matter. You're in that great seventh heaven or else in a hole as big as hell.'

He sat quiet; he had made up his mind that this was no time for him to talk.

'I was the great one for him too,' she said. 'Oh! yes, Ruth was the great one for him. Pretty soon we were going to be married. You've heard of being married? It's the thing girls are supposed to dream about all day.'

The bitterness of the words took him by surprise. He paused with a piece of ham half way to his lips and then immediately she surprised him a second time.

'By the way my name isn't really Ruth. But I'll have to explain about that later.'

Presently the car salesman discovered that he had very pressing business in Chicago; he would be back inside a week. She never saw him again.

'I daresay you think that expression about eating your heart out is a bit far-fetched but by the time I'd finished eating mine out you couldn't have fed a kitten on the scraps. There's a story I read somewhere once called *Out of Nowhere into Nothing*. That was how I felt. That was me.'

She went on living alone and working in the store. In her bitter necessity for companionship she totally rejected it. She became reclusive and sour, not speaking much to people. She described how she even got into the habit of biting her lips together before going to sleep at night, just in case, as she put it, she might be tempted to talk to someone in a dream.

'Not that I slept all that much,' she said. 'I was becoming a pill-eater pretty quickly.'

One afternoon, after about three months of this, Mrs Keller came into the store. She wanted a good sensible hat for travelling: a rain and shine hat, as she explained to the girl.

At the best of times Mrs Keller wasn't a very patient woman and the general behaviour of girls at store counters was something she didn't tolerate at all easily. But that afternoon something about the reclusive, shy-looking, pretty but rather tired-faced girl helping her to choose a hat seemed to her like a model of patience. She said several times how gracious she thought she was.

'Oh! and I mustn't forget another thing. That's important. She was wearing a big white orchid.'

Finally when the hat had been chosen and paid

for Mrs Keller did what seemed to be an extra-ordinarily kind, generous and charming thing. She unpinned the big expensive white orchid and handed it across the counter to the girl.

'You can wear it when you take in a movie with your boy-friend.'

The gesture was the first thing to do something to unlock the girl's long and reclusive silence and she said:

'That's very charming of you. I'll wear the orchid but there's no boy-friend.'

'Can't believe you haven't got one.'

'The past tense is never a very pleasant one. I'd rather not talk about it any more.'

Two days later Mrs Keller was back. She had been wondering, she said, if the girl would like to join her at dinner some time? She offered no explanation of this suggestion except that she thought it might be nice if they could spend a pleasant evening together. There was no mention of loneliness, no hint of any need for companion-ship, either for herself or the girl.

'In fact both of us were lonely.' Ruth Forbes fell suddenly into her old habit of biting her lips and once again stared down through the pine trunks, in one of her silences, at the sea. 'If any-thing she was lonelier than I was.'

After that they began to have dinner together quite often. They went to an occasional movie or theatre. They frequently went out to lunch on Sundays.

Once they had an interesting and, as it turned out, important conversation about travelling. It struck the girl as slightly odd that Mrs Keller, having taken infinite trouble to buy herself a travelling hat, should have done little or nothing in the way of travelling.

'The trouble is,' Mrs Keller explained, 'I can't really make up my mind about it. I can't make a decision. Have you ever done any travelling?'

'Occasionally on a bus.'

'My husband and I travelled to Europe for our honeymoon, but I'm afraid it didn't last very long.' Before the girl could make any comment on this Mrs Keller said: 'Do you feel you'd like to travel at all?'

'I suppose everybody would.'

'When I talk of travelling I mean a really long trip. A year or so.'

'I'd better start saving,' the girl said. 'At three dollars a week I might make two weeks in Rome by the time I'm fifty.'

Nevertheless the germ of the idea about travelling had been started in her mind and almost immediately she started saving: at first only minute sums every week and then bigger ones as she started economising on food, clothes, her fares and even cosmetics. It was a slow but obsessional process and its first importance wasn't so much that it succeeded in acquiring something of a nest-egg for her as that it helped greatly as an antidote to loneliness. Now she had something to look forward to; the out-of-nowhere-into-nothing mood slowly but completely evaporated.

Ruth Forbes fell again into one of her silences, sipping wine. Jack Marsden finished the last of the ham and chose one of his favourite figs, a big green one, as large as a good-sized pear. The cicadas seemed to whirr with an even greater and more frantic noon insistence as if not only they were quivering madly but every needle on every single pine. Once the sweet juice ran out of Marsden's fig and down his chin and he wiped it away and said:

'What made that honeymoon so short? You haven't told me that.'

'I know,' she said. She was looking down at the sea again; the golden brown pupils of her eyes seemed fuller than ever of tiny nervous veins. 'That's the crux of it all.'

'She bought me my first dress the day I was twenty-one.'

The meal was over; even most of the wine had gone. Jack Marsden and Ruth Forbes lay on their backs in pine shade that now, in the full heat of mid-afternoon, seemed to be less than that

76

of a ragged screen of lace. She spoke only after long intervals and seemed to have forgotten, for the time being, all thought of Mrs Keller's brief-lived honeymoon.

'It cost a lot of money. She'd been buying me little things before that – handbags, bottles of perfume, trinkets, bits of costume jewellery – you know the sort of thing. But this was the first real big buy.'

He was beginning to feel drowsy after the wine; her voice sailed away into the branches of the pine trees, sometimes to be utterly suffocated by the chorus of cicadas.

'She always said how pretty I was.'

'So you are.'

'Thank you. She always wanted me to have pretty things. She bought me a hat once. A little red straw. It had a fringe of black lace in the front. She couldn't have made more fuss about it if she'd been a man.'

He pondered on that remark, his mind growing drowsier every moment, for some time longer. It wasn't exactly that he detected anything sinister about it, merely that it seemed to have in it the shadow of something slightly repellent.

'Then she asked me to go and live with her, to share her apartment. Me in my rabbit hutch – you can guess what it meant. Hers was a four-roomed affair with velvet drapes and heavy carpets and two toilets and a view over the park. What would you have done?'

'Wrung her neck.'

'You've got to see this a little bit from her point of view—'

'What did you do? Did you go?'

'No. Not at first.'

'What did she say to that?'

'She didn't speak to me for a week. She was very cross. It was the first time I'd seen her when she hadn't been able to get her own way and she behaved like a vixen. I suppose I was awfully innocent but you could understand it really. I hadn't had much experience of possessiveness at that time.'

'I should understand a lot better if you told me about this honeymoon.'

'Yes.' She paused for some time and again her voice was almost smothered by the great sound of cicadas. 'Well, you see, there wasn't one.'

'You mean—'

'They went to Paris. They stayed one night. Then she came back alone. It just wasn't consummated.'

'Unlucky for her.'

'Oh! no, you've got hold of the wrong end of the stick. Unlucky for him. She was the one who wouldn't—'

'Ye gods and little fishes.'

She actually laughed, startling him so much that he came out of his half-doze to hear her say:

'It was really awfully funny. Awfully funny really—'

'Not my idea of fun!'

'Oh! what I mean was there was I pining away, eating my heart out because I'd been denied marriage and there was she with marriage in her hands and wanting to do nothing about it. The two of us were in the same boat but for different reasons.'

He lapsed into drowsiness again. He thought he heard a bird or an animal snapping a twig a little distance away but when he opened his eyes he saw that it was she walking about, packing up picnic things. She did this with methodical care, putting scraps of food into paper bags, wiping the beakers and finally putting everything neatly away into the basket.

'She had a farm up in the country too. We used to go there at weekends. There was a fair-sized lake near by, with trout in it and bass and things like that. She liked fishing. The first time I saw her dressed ready to go fishing she had heavy reddish check pants on and a thick blue flannel shirt and a leather belt and a wide-brimmed trilby hat. She was smoking a lot at that time. She smoked her cigarettes in a long brown holder and she looked like a man.'

The low insistence of her voice telling him all this put him into a complete and final doze. Once again he was asleep like a child, drugged by wine and heat and the shimmering voices of the cicadas.

How long he slept he didn't know but when he suddenly woke up she was no longer there. He jumped up and without stopping to think about it felt curiously alarmed. He was suddenly convinced that something, perhaps something awful, had happened to her. With this ridiculous notion firing him he ran twenty or thirty yards under the pines and then back again, calling her name. When she didn't answer he ran the other way, towards the road, and gave a shout in the direction of the sea.

A few moments later she came strolling back from behind a big clump of small bushes with thin laurel-like leaves and multitudes of small yellow flowers whose name at that time he couldn't remember.

'Oh! my God, where have you been?'

'Mr Marsden, what a question to ask a girl.'

He felt extremely foolish, said he was sorry and then found himself completely at a loss for anything to add. But suddenly he knew that he cared for her more than he had realised. He had really been scared of losing her. He had actually been alarmed for her physical safety.

'You wouldn't have liked it if I'd woken you up

to tell you I was going to pick daisies, would you?
You were sleeping like a baby.'

'Which I am.'

'Do you always sleep like that? There you were
one minute, listening to me, and the next you
were placidly dreaming. I talked for quite a bit
before I realised.'

'Did I miss something important?'

'Not really. I was sort of reminiscing. Are you
thirsty? I am.'

'Yes. I suppose it's the wine. We'll stop down on
the harbour and have a beer.'

He stooped to pick up the picnic basket and in
doing so caught sight of her bare brown legs. They
were good, elegant legs and a quick fire shot
through him. He let the basket stay where it was
and once again put his hands on her shoulders.
She didn't move. A strong temptation to caress
her breasts actually made him move his hands
downwards from her shoulders and then she said:

'It's been a nice picnic. Don't spoil it.'

'Kiss me.'

'I've already told you. I don't feel that way. It
isn't as easy as that—'

'One day I'll kiss you in a way you've never
been kissed before.'

'Is that a threat or a promise or what?'

'It's a statement of plain, warm human fact.
That's all.'

She said, with a slight touch of banter that gave sudden sparkle to the gold-brown pupils, that that was nice of him and that she wouldn't forget.

'Oh! and by the way – something else I mustn't forget,' she said. 'I remembered it while you were asleep.'

'And what's that?'

'You got an awful lot out of me but so far I've drawn a pretty good blank with you. You lure me on to strange islands, you swim with me at midnight, you take me on picnics, but who are you? Only God and Mr Marsden know.'

He laughed. 'Oh! me. I'm nobody. A promising junior executive in a paper-making firm who thought he'd like Greece for a month's holiday and now isn't sure.'

'Not sure? That's a fine compliment.'

'It is a compliment too. If it hadn't been for you I'd have gone home long ago. To hell with temples, ruins, gods, goddesses and the whole racket. Goddesses – I'll bet half of them had rickets and fallen arches. Not one of them could hold a candle to you.'

'Sometimes you say the very nicest things. Now what about that beer?'

She smiled. With one hand he picked up the picnic basket and with the other took her bare arm, holding it just above the elbow. The flesh was warm and very soft to the touch of his fingers.

He could feel the blood beating into the upper arm in strong pulsations, almost as if, at last, she were actually excited.

Once again a strong impulse to kiss and caress her went through him, but this time he checked it.

'Not yet,' his mind kept telling him, 'not yet.'

They drove back to the town. Dead silence imprisoned everything in a deep and sweltering vacuum. In the pitiless glare of sunlight all the flowers of the morning glory vines now sagged like airless rubber balloons, darkened from brilliant blue to an inky violet shade. Every chair outside every café was empty and only a cat or two moved along the harbour front among the boats, sniffing at some scrap of fish-gut or bone.

'I'm not only dying of thirst,' the girl said, 'but I'd like to freshen up a bit. What about trying that hotel over there?'

It struck Jack Marsden as a little curious that the small rose-walled hotel with bright orange shutters should have its name, *Acacia*, painted up in both Greek and English outside and he said:

'Looks clean, I'll say that. Anyhow we can try.'

At the side and a little to the back of the hotel a few chairs and tables were set out on a gravel courtyard under the shade of two big acacia trees. For ten minutes they sat there and waited and then at last Jack Marsden got up and went into the hotel and rang a push-bell at the foot of the stairs. The white and black marble floor struck almost chilly after the brutal heat outside.

After some two or three minutes' delay a big squashy woman, good-looking in a heavy sort of way, with friendly lips and huge black eyes, came out from the back of the hotel, giving a great involuntary yawn which flowered into a laugh as she tried to suppress it.

'Good afternoon,' he said. 'I don't know if you speak English, but may we have some beer?'

'Oh! yes I speak English. I learnt it in London after the war. You are from London?'

'About forty miles outside. I thought there must be a reason for having the name of the hotel put up in English as well as Greek.'

'It looks so nice in English, I think, don't you? Yes, we had a little Greek restaurant in Soho, and then my husband died. How many beers would you like please?'

'Two,' he said, 'and I should very much like to wash my hands.'

'If you will wait a moment I will bring you clean towels. The basin is at the end of the passage there.'

While she went to fetch the towels he unhurriedly washed his face and hands in a small stone basin fixed to the wall behind the stairs. Something about the small simple basin, the one tap, the clean cake of pink soap and the neatness of the red-and-white towels the woman brought him struck him as being very friendly.

'Perhaps you might even have known our little restaurant? Vlasopulos was the name.'

No, he confessed he hadn't known it. She smiled, friendly too, slowly unfolding one of the towels while she waited for him to finish swilling his face and hands. She was in fact actually holding the towel out for him as he finished and it was the sheer simple charm of this attentive gesture that suddenly made him say:

'Do you have rooms at all?'

'You mean now? Yes, I have rooms.'

'I am staying at the *Helios* at the moment,' he said, 'but—'

'They tell me it is very nice there. Would you perhaps wish to see the rooms? I could show you them gladly if you wished.'

'It was just a thought,' he said. 'I'll ask my friend.'

While Ruth Forbes went into the hotel to wash her hands he sat outside under the acacia trees, thoughtfully sipping beer, again oppressed by thoughts of Mrs Keller. The uneasy notion that she might be coming back had never really left him for very long all day. Now he was aware of his forebodings darkening rapidly again; he felt actually afraid of her coming back.

85

'I've just been thinking,' he said when the girl joined him again.

'Yes, what? It's very hot for thinking.'

'It was nothing much. It was just that I wondered if you'd like to change hotels.'

'Whatever put that into your head?'

'It was just a thought. She seems so very friendly, this woman. The place is so nice and clean—'

'You're not trying to tell me something, are you?'

'No,' he said. 'No.'

'Like you were getting bored again, I mean? If you don't want me here, if you'd rather I cleared out, you've only to say so.'

'It isn't anything like that at all.'

'No? I'd hate to be a burden to you. In fact I suppose I've been a hell of a burden already.'

Unprepared for this new flash of bitterness he sat staring at his beer, not knowing what to say. He dreaded she might suddenly recall the incident of the telephone call in the night. He half-wished he had been franker and had said 'It isn't that I'm bored, but I feel I'd like a change of scene, that's all. We could go to that place I mentioned before – what's its name? Kastoria. You know.'

'The beer's good and cold,' she said.

'Yes. I feel a whole lot fresher. But you didn't answer my question.'

'About changing hotels? No.'

'She has rooms all ready if you'd like to go up and see them.'

'Look,' she said. 'You change. I can see you want to change. I'll stay on at the *Helios*. You come over here.'

'Please,' he said. 'Let's just forget it.'

'You sow the seeds of all sorts of distrust into my head and then you just ask me to forget it. God, I wish I'd never come back. I was a complete fool to come back. I was crazy enough to think you were going to help me.'

'I'm trying—'

'Don't try any more,' she said and suddenly she got up, peevishly drained the last of her beer and walked into the street outside. 'I know when to pack my bag.'

# 8

They drove back to the *Helios* in complete silence; nor would she even look at him. Several times she ran her fingers through her hair, where the wind had ruffled it, but all the time she kept looking straight ahead.

It was only when they were walking along the beach, back to the bungalows, that he said:

'I suppose you know there's no way off this island until the next boat comes in? And I think that's the *Patria* a week from now.'

'I never gave it a thought.'

'Of course you could always swim.'

The joke, poor as it was, failed to raise even the ghost of a smile on her face and he said:

'Anyway why don't we swim? At least it'll cool us off a bit.'

'You might have something there.'

They swam, again in complete silence, and mostly thirty or forty yards apart. He felt keenly that she had become the complete stranger, peevish, bitter, irritatingly childish, deliberately cut off. His own temper was fretful too and the almost luke-warm water, with neither tang nor motion in it to freshen him, made him feel heavy and dispirited. Soon he found he lacked the energy to move his limbs and he slowly dragged himself out of the sea and sat on the steps of his bungalow verandah, not even bothering to dry himself.

All the time he sat there the house-martins soared continually across the beach, hovering and clinging to air outside the nest, nervous as ever, and once a wagtail appeared, prinking yellow across the shore above strips of burnt-up sea-weed, darting for flies.

Then the girl came out of the sea, running, shaking water from her hair, to astonish him completely. She was actually laughing when she reached him and he simply couldn't believe his ears when she said:

'Gosh, that was nice. That was marvellous. I feel a new person. That was what I needed all right.'

Before he could think of anything to say in answer to this sudden burst of what was almost gaiety on her part she ran into her bungalow to get a towel and came back almost immediately with it, a bright yellow one, and started drying her hair. He still couldn't begin to fathom her sudden and as it seemed almost deliberate change of mood and he simply sat watching the timid play of the hovering house-martins, wondering what on earth she would be saying next. And then, for the second time within a few minutes, she astonished him.

'I don't know what you thought of me this afternoon. But if I do it again just slap me.'

'Any particular place?'

'Anywhere you like. You have my full permission.'

She sat for some few minutes longer towelling her hair and occasionally dabbing drops of sea water from her brown shoulders. Once she leaned forward to dry her legs and he instantly caught a glimpse of the upper rim of her breasts, white as milk below the line of sun-tan. He could hardly have been more pleasurably startled if he had suddenly seen her completely naked. Something about that glimpse of pure whiteness, small though it was, started his blood racing and in another moment his mood too had changed completely.

'I accused you of being bored,' she suddenly said, 'and by gosh you've every right to be. You've got me to put up with. And that's enough to bore any man.'

'If you're trying to extract sweetness from the

more honied side of my nature you're going to be very unlucky.'

'That's right. That's the way to treat me.'

'I once knew a man who regularly slapped all his children before breakfast. In future that's what I'll do to you.'

'Good. I shall probably get to enjoy it enormously.'

'That,' he said, 'will probably be the prime object of the exercise.'

He kept a few bottles of beer in the bungalow and now he suddenly got up, went inside and came back with two opened bottles and two glasses. As he poured beer for her she slipped the bright yellow towel over her shoulders and he said:

'At the risk of being bored I want to ask you something.'

'I simply don't deserve another chance to make a fool of myself.'

'You certainly don't. But may I ask?'

'Ask away. I'm a sucker for anything.'

He gave her the glass of beer and then, before speaking again, poured his own.

'Well,' she said. 'I'm ready to be slapped.'

'It was just this, that's all. You said you'd tell me about your name,' he said, 'about not being Ruth.'

He never knew quite how soon or how long it

would be before she answered a question and now he was more than surprised that she answered quickly and with apparent ease.

'Oh! that was just before we caught the ship to come over here,' she said. 'We were standing in the baggage bay, looking at the letters above the bags – you know – when Beatrice suddenly said "I hope you won't take offence at this but I've never really cared for your name, Barbara. It's hard. It's altogether too hard for you. It really doesn't suit you at all." '

'What did you say to that?'

'I was taken by surprise and didn't know what to say. It didn't even remotely occur to me that I was about to be dispossessed of something – I suppose I was still awfully innocent in that way. I was also a bit hurt – it was rather as if someone had said they didn't like the colour of my hair or my eyes or something.'

'And then?'

'Then she went on to say that she always thought of me as belonging to a softer, more girlish name. She didn't think Barbara was at all feminine, not girlish at all. It wasn't just hard – it got shortened to Barb sometimes and that made it sound exactly like what it was – barbaric. No, she liked names that couldn't be shortened, like Ruth and Clare. She said Ruth would suit me fine.'

'You came by ship? I thought all you Americans were great ones for flying.'

'No, she hates flying. And I think that was significant too – I mean that she told me about the name and everything just before we got on the ship. She wanted the Barbara part of me to be left behind. She wanted to have me take on a new identity. So from then on it was Ruth. That's how it was.'

A boat came round the western headland of the bay, white, rather squat and with a small wheel-house, manned by two men in peaked yachting caps, with two girls as passengers. He remembered what the waiter had told him and thought that this, perhaps, was the boat he meant. One of the girls, with a scarlet scarf tied over her head, was sitting on top of the wheel-house and as the boat drew level with the bungalows she waved. The two men and the other girl waved too and Jack Marsden gave a casual wave in reply.

He was thinking that he didn't really care much for Barbara either and that for once Mrs Keller was right, Ruth suited her better, when she said:

'Unfortunately I couldn't get used to it very quickly. After all when you've been called Barbara for twenty-two years and just over it's a bit hard to change all of a sudden to Ruth.'

'Why didn't you object?'

'For one reason because I knew she'd go on calling me Ruth even if I did. I don't think you've quite got the measure of this awful persistence of hers. You don't know her well enough for that.'

Suddenly remembering the telephone call in the night, he made no comment at all.

'For another thing you've got to remember I wasn't in much of a position to object. I was taking the crumbs from off the rich girl's table. She was practically paying for the entire trip – my five measly dollars a week just about added up to a child's pocket money. It would have been pretty childish to have made a fuss.'

He thought he saw her difficulties. He sipped beer and kept quiet again.

'There were one or two incidents, though. The first day out we were promenading the deck when a girl and her husband went past and the girl waved and said "Hi, Barb? Having a good trip?" or something like that. She was a year or two older than I was and I'd known her casually at High School.'

The effect of this harmless incident on Mrs Keller was both violent and preposterous. She looked, the girl said, as if she'd seen the dead. Had he ever seen the face of a person on which almost entirely new skin had been grafted, so that it looked somehow like the skin of a dead fish left out to shrivel in the sun? That was how Mrs

Keller's face looked as the impossible rage about the incident struck her. Her skin turned suddenly a repulsive and unhealthy white. At the same time it shrank and the pores stood out, so that they looked almost like dry, flaky scales.

Then her guttural voice became locked in her throat. Imprisoned there, it choked as it tried to regain articulation and get out, so that it was nothing but an ugly barren rattle. In this speechless fashion she suddenly turned, stormed across the deck and went down to her cabin.

The girl gave her a quarter of an hour or so to calm down and then followed her to the cabin, only to find that it was locked. It was some time before Mrs Keller would let her in and when she finally did so a wreck of a woman, looking very nearly ten years older and almost ghoulish after battling against a flagellation of nervous exhaustion, sat on her bed, staring blindly through the stiffened fan of her fingers.

'I'll get you some codeine or something,' the girl said. 'Some aspirin. Have you some somewhere?'

Mrs Keller indicated a drawer in the cabin dressing table and then sank back on the bed, stiff as a line-prop falling down.

The girl opened the drawer and found a phial of aspirin among the usual clutter of lipsticks, scissors, nail-files and so on. She drew a glass of water from the wash-basin. And then in the act of turning to the bed her eye was caught by something else in the dressing table drawer: a small revolver.

It was the first time she had ever had any inkling that Mrs Keller carried a revolver and she hadn't much time to think about it or be surprised. Instead she got Mrs Keller to sit up, gave her several aspirins and held the glass of water for her to drink. After that she took off Mrs Keller's shoes, made her lie down again and pulled the coverlet over her.

Under these conditions the guttural rattle unlocked itself from the throat at last and became all at once caustically, terrifyingly articulate.

'If anybody ever calls you Barb again I'll shoot them. Barb! Listen to it. Barb! You might be calling a convict or a prostitute or something, not a girl like you. You're Ruth, I tell you. Ruth. That's how I think of you.'

When the girl had time to think of it the threat didn't seem by any means an idle one, simply born of rage. It still didn't fully occur to her that the imposition of this new identity of hers was something far more than the whim of a slightly eccentric woman who couldn't bear the sound of ugly consonants. She couldn't find any simple or rational explanation for it either, at that time, but the latent viciousness of the threat, coupled

D

with the ugly and irrational nature of the entire outburst, for the first time made her almost afraid.

But by evening it was all over. Mrs Keller was restored and calm again and by dinner time she couldn't possibly have been sweeter. And when she was sweet, as the girl was at pains to point out, no one could have been sweeter. All the generous side of her nature flowered again. She even went so far as to search her jewel-box and find a necklace which she took up to the dining saloon and produced at dinner, a peace-offering given with the sort of humility and grace it was impossible to resist.

'Go on, dear, please put it on. Wear it. It's topaz. It goes awfully well with your eyes. It's just your stone.'

That, the girl said, was how she got you. One minute she had you on the verge of hatred; the next she had you brimming over with pity. She charmed you to your knees.

By now the air along the beach had cooled a little; there was even a perceptible hint of an increase in the line of toy white waves breaking all along the deserted shore. Even so the evening was still enough for the sudden brash bray of a donkey to carry down from the hills a mile or more away.

'Do you remember the quarrel we had on board

the *San Philippa*? The one in the evening, at dinner?'

'Yes. I remember. I remember something she said too.'

'You mean you heard what we were saying?'

'It was the last thing she said before going out.'

'That I don't remember.'

'It's always stuck in my mind. "I have my own thoughts too," she said. I don't know – it somehow sounded—'

But what about the quarrel itself? he went on to ask her. What exactly did she mean?

'What would you think caused it?' she said. 'What sort of mighty incident?'

'Your wanting to run back home because you were suddenly getting afraid of a war?'

'Nothing so dramatic,' she said. 'She simply found me talking to one of the ship's officers.'

He poured out the last few drops of his bottle of beer and, while watching the foam rise and settle in the glass, waited for some fresh and more impossible revelation about Mrs Keller.

'That was a sin I also committed on the other ship. The third day out,' the girl said. 'I was actually attracted by a man.'

'And he by you. Very naturally.'

'Worse than that. I was silly enough to dance with him.'

'And what was the result of that?'

'Oh! she didn't rage, that time. She doesn't always rage. Sometimes she simply goes cold. You get the impression her blood freezes. A sort of mental rigor mortis sets in. And then she starts that sinister sarcasm.' He recalled suddenly that same sinister sarcasm on board the *San Philippa* – 'to you anything in the nature of a scrap of truth is sarcastic' – and once again all his fretful forebodings and misgivings came sharply crowding back at him.

'She called me cheap that day. You can't believe how she pronounces the word cheap until you've heard it. You might think she was calling you a whore.'

'I've never strangled a woman in my life yet,' he said, 'but I suppose there's always a first time.'

'You'd never have the heart to do it. She'd put you off by bringing you gold, frankincense and myrrh.'

'Blast her bloody soul! – that's all I can say.'

'That's a silly, useless threat, my dear man. She hasn't got one.'

He simply had to laugh at that. And perhaps, after all, he thought, that was the only thing to do with this impossible situation of preposterous trivialities – laugh it away, out of court, for ever.

'Come on, let's have one more swim. I tell you what. Ride on my back. I'll be your donkey. Your most humble beast of burden.'

'Nice thought. But I don't think I will. I'll sit a little longer. Look' – a martin swung and clawed at air and half-somersaulted, eager to get to the nest – 'the birds are coming home to roost now.'

He swam by himself. The day faded. A first star sent the faintest of signals from above a blackening headland, seaward to the east. He floated on his back, calm again now, thinking:

'Topaz? The ring was topaz, wasn't it, too?'

A few minutes later he was walking up towards the verandah, drying his hair with a towel. The girl, seeing him come out of the sea, got up from her chair and said:

'I must dress. It's getting dark already.'

'Tell me something—'

'Yes?'

It was on the tip of his tongue to ask her about the ring and then for some reason he decided not to; it was better she should tell him these things without prompting.

'What were you going to say?'

'Oh! it was just that – It was nothing – nothing at all—'

He broke off. A moment later as she started to move away to her own bungalow to dress he checked her by the arm for a few moments and lightly brushed her bare shoulder with his lips.

'You've got the nicest skin,' he said.

'Thank you.'

'It's just like the skin of a warm ripe plum. I'll bet those bow-legged goddesses never had a skin like yours.'

'No? What makes you so mad about those gods and goddesses?'

'Oh! I'm not mad. They're just not real to me. That's all. They're just *not*. They never were.'

She laughed a little, rather flatly.

'Don't be too sure. I get the feeling sometimes that they're around still. Playing with poor old gropers like us.'

'I decline to be called a poor old groper.'

'Like me then.'

'I won't have you called one either.'

On a sudden warm impulse he put his arm full round her body, just above the waist, pressing it affectionately. She was so taken by surprise that before she knew what was happening his fingers had touched the lower rim of her breast. The flesh was taut and firm and she actually made no movement to push his hand away. She seemed almost on the verge of some sort of acceptance of him. A new twist of excitement snatched at his veins and suddenly he turned her body full round to him with his free hand, still holding the lower edge of her breast with the other. It needed only the merest flick of his finger tips to strip the upper part of her swim-suit away and all his veins started racing. All she said was:

'Let me get dressed now.'

'There's plenty of time.'

Something made her look quickly over her shoulder and he said:

'Why are you looking over there? There's no one coming.'

'Nothing. It's just an old habit of mine.'

'Habit?'

'Yes. These old habits are hard to get out of. I suppose it's awfully silly but I just sometimes get the impression that someone is—'

'Following you?'

'Yes. If you must know.'

A moment later, the spell broken, she twisted out of his hands and half ran into the bungalow. He stood there for some minutes longer, staring at the sea, and it didn't occur to him until some time afterwards that she might have been frightened.

# 9

'You were the next offender,' she said. 'You committed the unpardonable sin. You took me off for coffee.'

'For Jesus' sake.'

It was nearly midnight; they were walking along the shore in the early smoky amber light of a moon that was coming up from beyond the mountain like a fat, over-ripe banana. At the word 'coffee' he was all of a sudden back along the quayside, eating honey and figs, on that first brilliant morning when the *San Philippa* had come in and he had the first of many impulses to stroke her as you might stroke a young and furry creature that hasn't quite grown up.

'I don't think you quite realised how glad I was to have you to talk to that morning. I was pretty desperate. I was very near the end of my tether.'

He watched the moon; its extraordinarily rich smoky amber was paling every second.

'Oh! yes and I might as well tell the whole truth while I'm at it. I did invent the cockroaches.'

'Knowing the *San Philippa* I shouldn't have thought that would have been necessary. I saw one as big as a mouse.'

'Please!'

He laughed and put his arm round her shoulder. She was wearing a pale blue dress of some light, almost transparent material and the upper sleeves were flouncy.

'I won't say I invented the war scare too. The papers were pretty grim, I thought. But I did invent the fact that I was scared. I just wanted to get home. I had to.'

'I'm sorry I mocked you a bit about that.'

'Oh! you didn't mock me. How could you know I was lying half the time?'

A fish leapt from the sea. Startled, she lifted her hand sharply and again gave that quick involuntary look over her shoulder.

'What was that?'

'Some old mermaid,' he said, 'tired of her underwater sink. Coming up for a look at the moon,' and was glad to hear her give an almost joyful peal of laughter in answer.

But soon she was quiet again; and then, after an interval, talking a little more. Had she said she was near the end of her tether that morning? What she should really have said was that she simply thought she was near the end of it. In fact she was a long, long way from it if she'd only known.

Then she started recalling the incident of her sun-glasses. He remembered that? – how, at the moment the boat sailed, she had dropped them into the sea. It was nothing less than sheer fright that made her drop them. She knew that she was in for another session, one of those awful sessions when the skin of Mrs Keller's face underwent the more odious of its transformations and became covered, as it were, with leprous scales.

It was some time, that morning, before she could bring herself to go down to her cabin. Another thing she perhaps hadn't ever properly explained about Mrs Keller was that somewhere in the central core of a personality that was very powerful anyway lay an extraordinary magnetism. It wasn't too much to say that it was almost hypnotic.

'Even when you knew it was going to be ghastly and sickening and unpleasant and everything else you felt you *had* to go to her. She somehow willed you there. Like some awful spider getting you. You *had* to go.'

'A scorpion. That's what she is. That's what she reminds me of. Now I know.'

It wasn't at all surprising therefore that when she finally pulled herself together that morning and forced herself to go below decks that it wasn't to her own cabin she went but to Mrs Keller's.

Mrs Keller was lying down on her bed. She didn't move or speak. The heavy slug of the *San Philippa*'s old, wearing engines underneath the cabin floor grunted like the pneumonic breath of a sick animal labouring up a mountainside. In some curious way it gave pain to the hot morning atmosphere and all at once the girl found herself the victim of that extraordinary quick-change emotional trick she had experienced about Mrs Keller so often before.

Suddenly she felt quite sorry for her. She leaned over and touched her on the shoulder.

'Don't touch me, you slut. Not *me*. Don't touch *me*.'

'Don't let's have a row, Beatrice. Not another. I've had nearly all I can stand.'

'Every day you get *cheaper* and *cheaper* and *cheaper* and *cheaper* and *cheaper* and *cheaper*!—'

'Beatrice, I can't take any more.'

'The passionate elopement.' The old sinister sarcasm came up from the bed in jets of vitriol. 'The ogling eye. Whistle and I'll come to you. What in God's name are you? A sex-starved imbecile?'

'I won't stand for this. Not any longer.'

'No, but you'll stand for the cheap trip. The

cheap pick-up. The cheap cup of coffee. The cheap stranger. The cheap anything so long as it's cheap.'

'Beatrice, I'm getting off the ship at Brindisi and going home.'

'You've no money. Even if you do it the cheap way you still haven't got the money.'

'I'll go to the Consulate. I'll manage somehow.'

'I'm sure you will. After all for a cheap rag like you there's always one way.'

It wasn't this most odious and final of insults so much as the loathsome and insistent repetition of the word cheap, uttered as only Mrs Keller could utter it, that finally drove the girl out of the cabin. And as she went she had a further unpleasant surprise.

On top of the dressing-table she saw the revolver for the second time. The fact that it was out of the drawer alarmed her so much that she actually ran from the cabin, trembling all over.

'I locked myself in my cabin for the rest of that day. I just lay there in the heat, listening to those awful thumping engines. I couldn't bring myself to think she was suicidal. It hadn't ever occurred to me. On the other hand I had to face it. Whichever way I looked at it I couldn't get it out of my mind. It was the worst day I could ever remember – apart from the one when I was so neatly jilted.'

'People who carry revolvers around are liable

to let them off,' he said. 'And if they don't get shot themselves somebody else often does.'

'Sometimes you have the most frightening way of going to the heart of anything. You seem to know what I'm thinking.'

On the slow, slogging *San Philippa* it was still another day after that to Brindisi. The next morning Mrs Keller and the girl met at breakfast and, as the girl remarked, there was no milk of human kindness in the coffee. Not a single word was spoken. For the first time there was no transformation scene. There was no attempt at reconciliation. Mrs Keller looked neither leprous nor odious; simply dead. The Teutonic-looking cheek-bones, already set unnaturally high in the face, seemed actually to have risen even higher in the night, leaving the jaws dropped and such flesh as there was on the cheeks grey and hollow. The eyes were utterly without life too. It struck the girl once or twice in fact that they had neither range nor focus. That eel-like oiliness that Jack Marsden later found himself hating so much had skinned the dark pupils completely over.

'I got back into another old habit of mine,' the girl said. 'I had to.' The two of them had walked their customary distance along the beach and were already walking back again, the moon white now over their right shoulders. 'Biting my lips like I used to do, so that I shouldn't speak. I felt if we didn't exchange a word everything might be all right. I could just leave the ship at Brindisi. But if we started speaking again I knew it would all flare up in the old, old way. And after all we had nothing to say to each other. It was all over.'

They walked another fifty yards or more before she spoke again; and when she did so she drew a great, difficult breath.

'But I was wrong. Just like I so often am.' She actually reached down and held one of his hands. 'We still hadn't got to the end. The worst part of all was still to come.'

'You remember the topaz necklace? About a week after that she gave me the ring.'

But this, she explained, was no ordinary gift; not this time. It wasn't one of those sweet gestures of hers, a kiss-and-let's-make-up affair. He'd find it hard to believe what she was going to tell him now and she hoped he would see it in the light of all that had happened before and that he wouldn't think her too much of a simple fool.

'She gave me the ring in France,' she said. 'At Fontainebleau. We'd been to see the palace there and afterwards we walked in the forest for an hour. It's very beautiful, that forest – I don't know if you know it – with hundreds of great beech trees. It's very special, somehow. You get the feeling of being in a big natural cathedral if you know what I mean.'

She supposed it was probably at its most beautiful in spring-time, but it was hard to imagine it being any lovelier than when she and Mrs Keller walked in it that day and all the beeches had begun to turn a fiery copper so that the air was absolutely saturated with just that same coloured light. There was a great hush over everything too, a sort of autumnal embalmment that made you want to talk in whispers if you wanted to talk at all. It was that cathedral atmosphere at its strongest and sometimes you got exactly the effect you often get in churches, when big shafts of light come pouring down through stained glass windows.

'It was pretty warm for late October too and after a while we stopped at a little kiosk sort of place where you could get drinks and a few things to eat. A family of children were playing rather noisily under the trees, picking up beech-nuts and I don't know quite how it was but somehow the conversation turned to children and Beatrice said did I ever think of marrying and having any and that sort of thing? I was still pretty bitter about the marrying idea at that time and I said No, I didn't want to, ever.'

This pleased Mrs Keller; she squeezed the girl's hand with uncommon affection, almost impulsively. Presently the children moved away and it was quite quiet again and the two of them were alone under the beeches, sitting on a bench at a table, sipping Vichy water. It probably didn't sound very special or romantic but somehow it was.

'And then all of a sudden she opened her hand-bag and took out the topaz ring. She didn't say anything. She just took the ring and spread out the fingers of my left hand and then put the ring on the third finger. I was too surprised to do anything about stopping her, which is what I ought to have done, and once the ring was on there wasn't a thing I could do. I was sort of trapped. I knew it and I felt pretty helpless.'

Did he think it sounded just plain stupid? Two grown women becoming engaged? Whether it sounded stupid or preposterous or impossible or not the fact is that's how it was. She was engaged to Beatrice Keller as surely as she'd have been engaged to Bill Shaw if he hadn't run out on her and let her down. And the funny thing was that in a queer sort of way, in spite of being trapped, she liked it at first. It made her feel secure. It sort of made her feel that whatever happened Beatrice wouldn't ever let her down. She would never let her get lost.

He hadn't once interrupted her as she told him all this, sitting with her legs curled underneath her in a chair at the olive tree end of the verandah, but something about the last sentence disturbed him unexpectedly and he was half ready to remind her once again about the idea of changing hotels when she went on:

'But what you have to understand is that it meant a great deal more than that to her. An awful lot more. I don't think I'd be putting it too high to say that she regarded us as being more than engaged. As far as she was concerned we were really married. It was for keeps. I didn't get that at first and when it gradually did dawn on me there wasn't a thing I could do about that either. She'd got me in her possession and pretty permanently at that.'

'But not now.'

The odd thing was that he didn't believe a word of this sentence, short though it was; he had begun to feel deeply, strangely uneasy again.

'Like you say, not now. God knows it might still be, though, if you hadn't asked me off that ship for coffee that morning. That started the break.'

'What ended it?'

'I made up my mind to get off the ship at Brindisi. I'd spend one night there and then see the Consul in the morning and try to borrow some funds. I'd fly home as cheaply as I could. Then something happened to make me change my mind.'

All that last day in the *San Philippa* the two women hadn't exchanged a word. A bitter and brittle pall hung between them and it wasn't until about half an hour before the ship docked that the girl decided to do the only civilised thing, as she saw it, and go to Mrs Keller to say good-bye.

'In fact it was a bit more than good-bye. It was separation – really I suppose divorce. Anyway I went along to her cabin. I always helped her pack – she wasn't very good at it herself – and there she was, in just about as hopeless a mess as you've ever seen. Clothes all over the place, nothing folded, nothing packed, everything in a God-awful state. And I suddenly felt sorry for her – I suppose I'm soft-hearted that way – and for two pins I'd have made it up again.'

Even then the two women didn't speak. The girl simply started to pick up a few things, fold them and put them into Mrs Keller's travelling cases. It was these last crucial few minutes of silence that neither of them would break that really decided things. A single word from Mrs Keller, a syllable or two of thanks for help with the packing, would have broken through the pall that had so bitterly separated them all day. But nothing came from Mrs Keller; she simply turned her back and stared through the porthole.

Finally when the packing was finished the girl said:

'It's all over, Beatrice. I'm flying home as soon as I've seen the Consul.' She took the topaz ring off her finger and laid it on the dressing-table. 'Here's your ring back. I couldn't keep that now.'

Mrs Keller turned sharply. She still had nothing to say and in fact there was now nothing she needed to say. All she might have said was cruelly frozen in her face.

'She looked insane,' the girl said. 'I've never seen a face like it. It was a face of the damned.'

Even then they drove to a hotel together. Still in silence, they booked separate rooms and went upstairs. The girl freshened herself up a bit, changed her dress and took a couple of aspirins in a glass of water. It was already growing dark outside. It seemed as if a storm might be brewing up. She hated storms and thunder but even so she decided a walk and a breath of air would do her good. She hadn't eaten much all day and even now she really wasn't hungry.

She opened the bedroom door to go out and there, outside, stood Mrs Keller, still with that frozen and insane look on her face, exactly as if she'd been standing there for hours.

'She said could she come in for a moment and I said "Yes" and she came in. She shut the door and stood there for a good half minute, staring at me. Then I woke up to the fact that she'd got the revolver in her hands. "I'm going to kill you," she said, "and then finish myself." '

'My God!—'

'Oh! she meant it all right. A couple of seconds more and she'd have pulled that trigger. And then a bit of the pattern fell into place.'

'Pattern?'

'You remember how I asked you if you thought there was a pattern in all this and you said yes, you were beginning to think so.'

'I remember.'

'Suddenly there was the most God-awful clap of thunder. One of those real big sudden ones that leap out straight overhead and frighten you to death. It certainly frightened me but not half as much as it scared Beatrice. She practically dropped the revolver as she jumped and in a second I knocked it out of her hands and kicked it under the bed. I think I must have kicked her too – I really can't quite remember—'

Partly because he was still uneasy, partly because he realised that she needed some sort of gesture of comfort, he got up out of his own chair and went over to hers. She was still sitting with her legs curled up underneath her. She had slipped off her shoes and her bare arms were loose on the sides of the chair.

'You must have thought it awfully odd of me to send that telegram and then turn up like that, but now you see how it was.'

'Listen, shall we change hotels tomorrow?'

'If that's what you'd like to do.'

For a single second the leprous face of Mrs Keller appeared to stare at him out of the moonlight but he smothered it aside, as he hoped, for ever.

A few moments later he held the girl tenderly by the upper arm and kissed her full on the mouth; and this time, except that she stirred with a deep tremor, like a child coming out of sleep, there was no kind of protest at all.

It must have been nearly two o'clock before he finally said good night to her. At the last moment he kissed her fondly again and said 'Sleep well' and she said in return:

'Sleep well. Have good dreams. Sleep well.'

'Me?' He laughed quietly. 'Sleep well? Never do anything else. Can't ever remember missing an hour's sleep in years.'

'Lucky man,' she said.

He at last went into his bungalow, undressed, took a long drink of cold water and got into bed. He gave a customary deep breath, shut his eyes and was calmly asleep within a minute or so.

It was probably more than an hour later when he started to dream with torturing brilliance that Mrs Keller, like some evil spider crawling out of a hole, was sitting on the end of his bed, the revolver in her hand, watching him. The reality of all this was so great that he could actually hear her guttural breath grating in a curious way in her throat, giving two sharp hard notes and then a pause. He could see with chilling and frightening clearness the high Teutonic cheek-bones, the flaky skin, the smeary orange lips and the eyes that had never lost for him that first impression of eel-like oiliness. The air of the room was choked with an unclean cloud of hatred and a suspense of all movement that was more terrifying than any movement could possibly have been. Exactly like a patient and odious spider coiled in the centre of its web she sat there waiting to pounce at him when the final moment of execution came.

He started moaning heavily in his sleep, at the same time trying desperately to run. As the moaning grew stronger his legs got heavier and weaker, holding him back. Suddenly in the middle of one of his more desperate efforts to lift his legs off the ground he saw her slowly get off the bed, turn herself full face to him and lift the revolver, pointing it directly at him.

In a fit of choking despair he gave a final tormenting groan and threw out his arms, trying to clutch the back of the bed. The sheer desperation of the movement immediately woke him up and the next thing he knew he was half-kneeling, half-lying on the floor, his hands locked over the top of his head in the act of warding off an impending blow. His lips were still blubbering with fright and his whole body was chill and stiff with a paralysis so complete that it was several minutes before he could get up off his knees and grope his way to find the light switch.

Even then his fear was still strong enough to make him almost leap for the switch and turn with terrified sharpness as the light came on, fully expecting to see Mrs Keller still sitting on the bed. His relief that she wasn't on the bed was even greater than his fright had been and he at once threw himself down on the bed, holding his face in his hands.

He might have been lying there for almost five minutes before he was struck by another strange impression. It was that he could still hear that guttural breathing of hers, low, distinct but now much farther off: the same repetition of two sharp notes and then a pause. It had something of the effect of a signal, curiously metallic and monotonous, trying to send him a message, a warning of some approaching catastrophe.

He managed to pull himself together at last and stood in the centre of the room, listening. He then realised suddenly that the sound had nothing to do with Mrs Keller. It wasn't in the room either. It was distinctly coming from some distance along the shore.

He slipped on a pair of canvas shoes and went out to the beach. The moon, though waning and setting, was still strong enough to illuminate the shore and half-way between himself and the hotel he could clearly make out the shape of a rowing boat drawn up on the sand. A solitary figure was bending over the boat and now and then that brief duet struck the air, two sharp taps and then a pause.

He started to walk along the beach, very slowly at first, still not quite himself, his legs heavy and the chill on his flesh still strong. The experience of seeing Mrs Keller sitting there on the end of the bed, ready to shoot him, was still so powerfully with him that once or twice he gave a sudden brief shudder and involuntarily fell into that old habit of the girl's – that of turning sharply, very much like a frightened child, to see if anyone were following him.

When at last he got as far as the boat, still in this unsteady state of mind, he immediately recognised with great relief that the figure bending over it was his friend the talkative waiter. By the light of the moon he was hammering at something on the gunwale of the boat with a round white stone.

'Ah! good evening, sir. You can't sleep tonight?'

The face of the little waiter, normally pinched, dark, contemplative and rather sad, looked even more so in the yellow light of the setting moon. It might even have been that he too had had a vision of Mrs Keller.

'I just heard this noise and wondered what it was.'

'I bent one of my hooks and was just trying to straighten it out. I hope I didn't waken you, sir?'

'No, I wasn't asleep. Just going out? or have you been?'

'Just going out, sir. Trying to get something for breakfast.'

The very early morning air, though still warm, was clearer and fresher than Jack Marsden could remember it and he took several good deep breaths of it as he stood watching the waiter hammer out the hook. The breaths of air had the effect of cleansing his mind and he said:

'Good fish here?'

'Not bad, sir. The water's too warm for really good fish. Still, they're all we have.'

The waiter gave the hook a final hammering with the stone, then picked it up and held it up in the moonlight. It was a fair-sized hook and the hammered tip of it shone gold for a moment before he said:

'That ought to do. Can't afford to lose hooks. Too expensive.'

He threw the hook into the bottom of the boat with the rest of his tackle and then started to push the boat down to the sea. Jack Marsden put his weight on to the boat too, helping to push, and the waiter said:

'Thank you, sir. If you can't sleep why don't you come out for an hour? It's very calm out there. Very restful. As good as sleeping.'

It didn't need a final shadow of Mrs Keller's spirit sitting back there in the bungalow to make him decide. The great tranquillity of the night was enough to make him say 'Good idea' and cock a leg over the side of the boat at the moment it floated.

'Like me to row?' he said. 'Then your hands will be free.'

'That's very good of you, sir.'

He started to row slowly and easily towards the centre of the bay. There were many stars of great brilliance and he watched them as he rowed. The sea was still without so much as a ripple on it and there was no sound except that of the oar-blades dipping and stroking the water and the occasional plop of the waiter's line as he cast it out.

After he had rowed about half a mile the waiter said:

'No need to go much further, sir. It's all much the same, this bay.'

He stopped rowing, shipped oars and sat watching the waiter fish. Now and then he made a sudden strike but nothing much ever happened and finally Jack Marsden said:

'Your luck doesn't seem to be in much tonight. Is it always like this?'

'Sometimes better. Sometimes worse. But it doesn't really matter to me. I come for the ride. For the quietness.'

'You come every night?'

'Every night.'

After about forty minutes he struck hard and caught his first fish, a whitish, rather stumpy one, thick across the middle, about nine or ten inches long. He took it from the hook and without much visible enthusiasm, looked at it for some moments as if wondering whether to throw it back or not and then dropped it into the bottom of the boat, where it flapped about, gasping.

'Two or three more like that and you'll have a good breakfast. Your wife will be pleased.'

'Not married, sir. I share them with the other waiters.'

Jack Marsden laughed but he noticed that the waiter didn't laugh in reply.

'Plenty of girls, though, I expect,' he said. 'Waiters always have plenty of girls.'

'No girls, sir. Not me.'

After that he fished for a long time in silence. The surface of the dead calm water was broken now and then by a sharp strike or two and once he struck harder and sooner than usual and the surface of the water exploded white in the falling darkness.

'That was a big one,' Jack Marsden said.

'Too big for me, sir. I don't like them too big.'

Presently he caught three or four smaller fish, which pranced and flapped wetly about in the bottom of the boat, expiring. And then, as he baited up another hook, he suddenly said:

'I had a girl until last year. There's a little village up there where I showed you the monastery. She came from there.'

He cast his line out; it whisked across the air, still pale with waning moonlight, like a spider's thread.

'She was fifteen. Her mother wouldn't let us marry. She was too young, she said.'

'I thought Greek mothers liked their daughters to marry young.'

'Not this one. She wanted to keep her. She didn't want no one else to have her. Ever. At all.'

He drew in his line; the bait had vanished. He re-baited the line and threw it out again.

'I said I would run away with her. If there's
something you don't like you have to run away
from it, I say. I used to think it was cowards that
run away, but not no more. It's the wise ones who
run away.'

Presently he had another fish on; it too flapped
with the others in the bottom of the boat.

'We were going to run away one Sunday. I have
a sister in Piraeus and we were going to her. Then
the boat didn't come in – engine trouble again,
always with those old boats, engine trouble.'

'They should sink the lot.'

'So she came down from the village on Monday.
In the bus. There'd been a storm the night before,
with plenty of rain. Plenty of rocks coming down
too. Big ones. On the road. Everywhere.'

By now the moon had set completely, but
already, on the opposite side of the bay, the merest
break in the night sky was showing in a low grey
line.

'It was a very big rock that bus hit. Three times
as big as this boat. It fell right over a cliff. Right
down. Fifteen of them were killed.'

Jack Marsden didn't say anything. He watched
for some time the half-dozen fish in the bottom of
the boat, some dead by now, some still feebly
flapping, and at last heard the waiter say:

'That was when I started to come out here
in the boat. I don't think so much about her

out here – well, not in the same way. The sea seems to take care of her. You understand what I mean?'

He said he thought he understood. Yes, he could understand about the sea.

'You can bring the bad things out here and drown them, sir, that's how I mean.'

He sat quiet, looking at the waiter baiting another hook, not answering this time. If there was any increase in the sadness on the face of the waiter it was also touchingly calm. In turn it induced a new sense of calmness into Jack Marsden, driving out the last shadow of Mrs Keller's evil spirit. Over and over again he could hear the waiter's words revolving through his mind – you can drown the bad things, sir, and it's the wise ones who run away – so that finally he sat there secure in a decision about Ruth Forbes. He felt he fully understood her now. The frightening vision of Mrs Keller had thrown up into awful relief far more than anything she had been able to tell him herself, all her own complex nightmare. He knew now how she had been driven beyond endurance into a state when she too must have been half crazy.

It was time to ask her to marry him, he thought. In thinking this he also thought suddenly of the girl the waiter had lost. His calm left him for a moment, to be replaced by a vivid moment of panic in which he felt Ruth Forbes might even now be lost to him too. At the same time he realised how rapidly it was growing daylight. He looked at his watch and saw that it was nearly six o'clock and said:

'It's later than I thought. I suppose we ought to be getting back soon.'

'Yes, sir. I think so too.'

He started to row back across the bay and presently the waiter said:

'Perhaps you would like to have some of the fish yourself, sir, for breakfast?'

'Oh! no thanks. You have them for yourself. You've earned them.'

'I would like you to have some, sir.'

'Oh! I couldn't, thanks. A hungry man like you can deal with that lot in no time.'

'Perhaps your lady would like to try some, sir? Even if you won't.'

There was something so touching about this remark that Jack Marsden, looking sharply up at the waiter's face, saw that it was no longer merely sad. It was deeply hurt; it wouldn't have surprised him at all to see a hint of tears in the small dark eyes. He at once felt bitterly reproachful of himself and said:

'I'm sure she would. We'll ask her. I know she'll be delighted.'

'That's fine, sir. I'll get one of the cooks to do

them nicely, sir. Just grilled, in butter. With lemons.'

The sudden happiness in the waiter's face was so great that Jack Marsden could hardly look at him. He simply stared eastwards, towards the sun and the mountains that sometimes looked almost barbaric but that now had the appearance, in the rising light, of long folds of deep brown velvet stretched softly across the sea.

Half an hour later the boat was on the beach and he was watching with astonishment the figure of Ruth Forbes running down from her bungalow. She was wearing a pale yellow housecoat over her nightdress. It was loosely and hastily tied and as she ran he could see her bare sun-brown legs gleaming in the sun.

There was something so exciting about this that he could think of nothing to say until she called:

'Heavens, you had me worried. I looked in your room and you'd gone. Gosh, I thought you'd left me. Where have you been? Couldn't you sleep for a change?'

'No.' Slipping his hand round her waist, he bantered quietly: 'I just had immortal longings in me for once, that's all.'

'Longings? For what?'

'Fish for breakfast,' he said, laughing, and kissed her lightly on the neck.

For a few moments the sad face of the waiter

E                                               129

broadened with laughter. As if with answering delight the chorus of cicadas rose with greater shrillness in the olives. Something suddenly made Ruth Forbes laugh too. And with tenderness he looked down at her face and said:

'I've been watching the stars. Do you believe in the stars?'

'In a way I think I do.'

'I'm glad,' he said, 'because today they're going to be very good for you.'

# 10

Next day he drove to the other side of the island with something more than an ordinary sense of relief; and presently this in return gave way to a new excitement.

He suddenly felt that he was seeing the little town and its harbour with an entirely fresh pair of eyes. The boats, the fishing nets hanging out to dry, the blue trumpets of the morning glory vines, a stall with a woman selling hats, even a man with a pair of big black moustaches selling ice-cream: since his last visit all of it seemed to have been painted and varnished over to acquire a sparkling and trembling brilliance in the sun.

At the Hotel Acacia Madame Vlasopulos gave them two rooms at the back, the cooler side. When the big wooden shutters of the windows were open in the morning it was possible to see for a good distance across the mountains. A white string of road ran across and into them and finally disappeared, several hundred feet up, into an arrow-head of cypresses. While the many olive trees that spread all across the lower slopes seemed to heighten the impression of great heat the cypresses looked dark and cool.

The following day he and Ruth Forbes drove into the mountains, again taking a picnic, with wine. On the lower reaches of the road vines spilled over crumbling walls, with blue morning glory flowers and pink geranium sometimes mixed among them. Fig trees of great age flopped leaves like huge ears under perpendicular oleanders, rosy with prodigious flower. There were again many mulberry trees, not very large but heavy and black with fruit, and here and there a few young orange and lemon trees. Then as the road rose steeply, climbing out of the first rich hundred feet or so of coast, the trees thinned, leaving nothing but ancient olives clawing among great rocks, black-armed and grotesque, a few scattered pines and, on the roadside, many small-leaved bushes covered with light creamy-yellow flower.

Marsden remembered seeing these bushes before and said: 'I told you how bad I was at names but I ought to know the name of that flower. I've seen it before and it bothers me.'

'It's news to me that you're a botanist.'

'Well, not exactly. My father was very keen.

We used to take long walks together when I was a boy and he'd teach me the names of trees and flowers and things. Then if I got tired he'd kid me on by offering me a penny for every tree I could name. Things like that stick – that's how I come to know.'

That morning she was wearing an apricot-coloured blouse, open at the neck, and pale green shorts and a white and green head-scarf to keep off the sun. Now and then the breeze made by the movement of the car caught the head-scarf and tore at it with a sharp flap. Whenever this happened she turned her head quickly and he turned in response too, smiling and trying to fathom the response behind the dark sun-glasses.

Just before midday they got as far as the cypresses. In blistering heat and to the customary delirium of cicadas they unloaded the picnic things and Jack Marsden put the two wine bottles behind a cypress trunk, in the blackest part of the shade. Then he asked her if she wanted to eat at once or if she would like to wait a little and cool off first and rest. She took off her head-scarf and sun-glasses and wiped a few beads of sweat from under her eyes and said:

'Let's rest a bit. I'd like a drink of mineral water too if you remembered to bring it. Did you?'

'Damn. It's in the back of the car. Probably boiled by now.'

By the time he had found the mineral water and two glasses she was lying down flat in the shade. She sat up at the sound of the water being poured and said it was good, that sound. He gave her a glass and she drank and then said:

'It's still pretty cool too. For a wonder.'

'Goes down jolly well.'

'Jolly – I love that word. Remembered the name of your flower yet?'

'Not yet. But I will. It's this heat. It fries my brains.'

'I like it. It never really bothers me.'

She finished the rest of the water and lay down flat again, staring up into the overhead mass of cypress branches. For some time longer he sat watching her, taking occasional gulps of water until at last his glass was empty. Then he went and sat much nearer to her and suddenly said:

'Madam, I've got news for you.'

'Pleasant, I hope?'

'I hope you'll think it is.'

'Well?'

He waited a few moments before answering. The entire blistered mountainside seemed to quiver with the delirious beat of cicadas and after listening a few moments longer he said:

'I'm afraid I've got to be back in England next week.'

She suddenly sat up as if startled.

'What did you say? Pleasant?' He wasn't quite sure if she were joking or serious now. 'Is this a polite way of telling me you're leaving me in the lurch or something?'

'No, madam.'

'I wish you wouldn't call me madam. It sounds as if you're trying to mock me.'

'My God, I wouldn't mock you for anything. Not for anything in the world. No, in case you're still listening it's just my way of asking if you'll marry me.'

For almost a minute she sat staring at him without a word, eyes completely blank. Then very much to his surprise she lay down again, this time on her side, staring away from him.

'You shouldn't frighten a girl like that.'

'Frighten?'

'Yes, frighten.'

'You mean to say it came as a surprise after the way I kissed you last night?'

'It isn't just that it's a surprise – it's because it's so altogether different from everything that's been happening to me lately.'

'That I can understand.'

He lay down beside her and kissed her quietly several times on the mouth.

'Tell me what you feel about what I said. I'd like to take you to England.'

'I don't feel anything.'

'No?'

'No, it's quite painless, thank you,' she said and smiled.

He smiled back at her. He suddenly felt not only extraordinarily happy himself but he thought that for the first time she was undeniably happy too.

'I think the *Patria* comes in on Sunday and goes back to Athens. We could fly from there. I'll find out about it in the morning.'

'That gives us two more days.'

'I'd like to get the ring in London. As soon as we get there we'll go out and get lost in the fog and I'll put it on your finger in the park.'

'Sometimes you say the nicest things. Is it always foggy in London?'

'Oh! always. Dense. Winter and summer. That's what makes the English so aloof. The fog completely cuts them off from each other.'

'Now you're teasing me again.'

'I only tease you to make you happy. Are you happy?'

'I've never been so happy,' she said, 'for a long, long time.'

He kissed her again, still very quietly, still the very slightest bit afraid that any rush of emotion might destroy the stability of confidence it had been so hard to build up in her, and finally she smiled again and said:

'This is the first time I ever knew that kissing can make you so hungry. I'm ravenous.'

'Hunger and love,' he said. 'Yes, that's right. The one stimulates the other. Let's have lunch then.'

'Yes, let's do that,' she said.

Several times during lunch she confessed that the wine was making her drowsy. She hadn't been sleeping well lately. Not in fact for weeks and weeks and weeks.

'You should get hold of a bad book and read that for a while. There's nothing like a bad book for curing insomnia.'

'Do you happen to have any bad books with you?'

'I've got the best bad book ever with me. It's Baedeker's *Greece* for 1896. One page will put you away for keeps.'

'Why 1896? You must have been very young then.'

'Oh! I picked it up cheap. They were the days to travel. You lived for a penny a day and they cut your throat into the bargain.'

'Which made it cheaper still. I must borrow this fascinating book tonight.'

'You must. I won't forget to find it for you.'

After lunch she lay down again and in a very few minutes her eyes were closed. He sat for some time longer looking at her as she dropped with complete tranquillity into sleep, her face utterly relaxed, all trace of tension gone. Sipping the rest of the wine, he felt once again, for some reason, poised in a vacuum, every trace of his own misgivings and anxieties finally dispersed and shut away. He even discovered that he could at last think of Mrs Keller without either odium or anger. Even his dream of her no longer troubled him.

Some time towards mid-afternoon he left her sleeping in a state of almost miraculous peacefulness under the cypresses and took a short walk up a hillside path under the trees. The air, he thought, had grown more impossibly oppressive than ever since lunch time. The heat was like boiling glue; a thick threat of thunder filled the air. Across the bay, for some distance above the mountain horizon, a band of vaporous coppery yellow had formed, almost sulphurous, and he got the impression that it might suddenly ignite spontaneously. He even thought he once detected the first faint crack of thunder, like immensely distant artillery, across the farthest hills.

He started to walk back. To add to the oppressiveness of the air the rather over-sweet scent of the small bushes of yellow flowers floated everywhere. And all at once, in a swift moment of recollection, he remembered what the shrub was.

'Myrtle. Of course. I was reading about it on

the boat. In a guide book or something. Probably the Baedeker.'

He stopped and broke off two or three boughs of flower. The scent of them made him feel almost drowsy himself. The rather soporific idea went through his head that he had read somewhere, perhaps in a guide book, too, that the shrub, the myrtle bough, was sacred to somebody or other, one of the gods or goddesses, Venus perhaps, but it was all rather vague and in the oppressive heat he was incapable of thinking clearly and couldn't exactly place it.

When he got back to the girl she was still sleeping quietly. He got himself a drink of mineral water, now unpleasantly luke-warm, and then sat down again, feeling a drowsy satisfaction at merely watching her sleeping. All the time he was twisting the sprays of myrtle round and round in his hands and now and then he could have sworn, once again, that he heard the distant crack of thunder.

She opened her eyes at last and simply lay there, still half-drugged with sleep, looking up at him without a word. He smiled at her and in a long-delayed response she said:

'I've had such a beautiful sleep and I've been an awful long way away somewhere. I think it was London – but I wouldn't really know because I've never been there.'

'Was it foggy?'

'No. Bright, bright sunshine.'

'Then,' he said, 'it couldn't have been London. No fog? The English would never live the slander down.'

Again she lay quietly looking up at him and again, after a long delay, she spoke and said:

'Did I dream it too or did you ask me to marry you?'

'Unless I'm very much mistaken I did.'

'And what did I say?'

'Apart from saying it was quite painless you didn't say much one way or the other.'

'Please forgive me. Please may I still say Yes?'

She involuntarily flung up her arms in a gesture of sudden emotion, with a little cry, and pulled him down to her. She held him in the crook of her arm, closely, her mouth pressed against his face, in a sort of trance, and it was only after a long time that she roused herself with a deep sigh that was almost a shudder and said:

'What have you got there in your hands?'

He explained that it was the shrub they had talked about earlier on and how he had now remembered its name.

'Myrtle. I always think it's got something classical about it. Like acanthus and asphodel. Only asphodel's such a terribly disappointing flower.'

'And here's me hardly knowing a carnation from a rose.'

'Venus comes into it somewhere. I think it was sacred to Venus.'

'You and your flowers and goddesses. Here's a very happy girl absolutely out of her depth.'

By this time he had twisted the two or three sprays of myrtle into a rough sort of ring and on a sudden impulse he leaned down and put it on her head like a crown.

'The only ring I can give you for the moment. Will it do?'

'Sometimes you do the very nicest, nicest things to me. Thank you, darling, very much.'

It was the first time she had called him this and in an instant he could have sworn there were tears in her eyes. Again she lifted her arms. The crown of myrtle slipped from her head and again she drew him down to her. Without any hesitation he kissed her full on the mouth, holding first one of her breasts and then the other in his hands. Her body quivered sharply in response, but there was no protest, and presently he slipped his hands into the neck of her blouse. As he touched the naked breasts she turned her body sharply away and then just as sharply back again. Then he bent down and kissed first one breast and then another and soon she was lying there staring at him with a great look of wonder in her eyes.

'You must have thought me very odd all this time,' she said. 'You must have thought me a very difficult and awkward sort of creature. But you see I just don't know about all this. It's never happened to me. I just don't know.'

She drew him down to her again and they lay for a long time in the oppressive, steamy shade. Once, from no great distance away, a rock cracked in the heat, fell and went bouncing with a series of pistol-shot leaps into the dry gorge below. Then, far off, these small disturbances seemed to make far louder echoes that crumped, like a string of bombs, across the sea. He heard it clearly and this time there was no mistaking it – he knew it was the sound of thunder.

She heard it too and said sharply:

'That wasn't thunder, was it? I hate thunder. I can't bear thunder.'

'No: just the gods muttering.'

'Don't tease. I hate thunder.'

'It was a rock falling. Didn't you hear it go?'

'I hate being alone if there's thunder. I just can't bear it. The sound always seems to hit me between the eyes and make my head ache so.'

'No need to be afraid of thunder. It's the lightning that kills.'

'You shouldn't have said that.'

'I could cut my tongue out. It was a very, very stupid thing to say.'

She started sharply and broke away from him.

'There it goes again,' she said. 'I heard it clearly that time. There's no mistaking thunder. We ought to go.'

'No. Don't let's go. Not yet.'

Suddenly she broke away from him completely and stood up. He stood up too and for another single minute she stood there in an indecisive sort of trance, the neck of her blouse fallen away, her breasts partly exposed. An impetuous wave went rushing through all his veins and he said:

'Don't go. Make love with me before you go. Don't go – not yet.'

'Not here,' she said. 'There'll be another time. I promise you there'll be another time.'

'I want you terribly now.'

'I know you do. And don't you think I want you too? But not here – not now. I can't bear that thunder.'

He had sense enough not to insist that she stayed. She dressed and with something like agony he watched her two breasts, firm and very white against the deep sunburn of her neck and shoulders, and tenderly rose-brown at the tips, disappear into the blouse. The thunder crackled again even while she was dressing and suddenly she held his face in her two hands, kissed him briefly and said:

'Where did my crown of myrtle go? I want to take it with me.'

By nine o'clock that night the storm, like some enraged hound of the gods, had finally released itself from the mountains and was barking with a grand viciousness over the town. As lightning forked the rainless sky every few minutes or so the girl sat in the little hotel dining room drinking cup after cup of coffee, arms crooked on the table, hands actually trembling, until at last she said she could bear it no longer.

'I'd be happier in bed,' she said, 'with that bad book of yours.'

She presently went upstairs and he followed her after a few minutes, going to his own bedroom to find the book for her. The big double shutters of the bedroom windows were closed, completely shutting out every trace of lightning. He undressed, put on his dressing-gown and then went to take the book to her.

She was sitting up in bed in her nightdress, a coffee-coloured one with a wide loose neck.

'You can't see the lightning at all with the shutters closed,' he said. 'I brought the book.'

She smiled and looked up at him and again the look on her face was one of great wonder, incredibly without a trace of fear.

He put the Baedeker on her bed-side table and sat down on the bed.

'The old Baedeker's a very poor excuse I'm afraid,' he said.

'Did you need an excuse? I said there'd be another time.'

For answer he took hold of her nightdress and pulled it over her head. She sat there completely naked and a moment later he slipped off his dressing-gown and got into bed and lay down beside her.

He kissed her, holding her breasts again, and she said:

'Remember what I told you. I don't know about this. You'll have to teach me about it all – it isn't easy for me after all that's happened—'

'Forget that now,' he said. 'That's all over and done with now.'

The storm raged and crackled with a sudden fresh burst of fury that made her draw deeper down into the bed, taking him with her.

'Yes,' she said. 'It's all over now. Thank God it is too.'

But, as he was to discover the following morning, it was not all over.

# I I

The storm, hot and noisy but always without rain, kept them awake until the early hours of the morning and they slept late, neither of them waking before eleven.

He woke first and for some time lay looking at her in the morning half-light. She had thrown the covers back and her sun-burned shoulders and part of her breasts were bare. She looked happy and relaxed in sleep. The corners of her mouth were not drawn down, as they had often been before, and there was something quite childlike about the soft, steady, barely audible breathing.

When she woke at last, quite suddenly, she smiled and said:

'I knew someone was watching me. So it's you, is it?'

'Yes, it's me. The man in your bed.'

'You've led me into very bad ways.'

'And you look so unhappy about it. What about some breakfast? I can smell coffee.'

'You're in bed with me in what is known as a very compromising situation and all you think about as usual is eating and drinking.'

'Naturally. Love makes you hungry, as I told you yesterday. Don't you want breakfast?'

'No, I want love.'

'I'll have breakfast and then come back and you can have all the love you need.'

'Disgusting, selfish man.'

'Besides, there's another thing. I have to call the shipping agency to find out what time the *Patria* goes on Sunday and if we can get berths.'

'Berths? You make a dishonest woman out of me and then talk about berths.'

'Fair enough. I'm sure they'll have a double berth. If not we can always sleep on deck.'

He started to get out of bed but she looked at him with special fondness and held him back against her, pleading with both her mouth and eyes for him to stay with her a little longer.

'Kiss my breasts again. The way you did last night. The goddesses never got themselves kissed like that – not in a thousand years.'

When he finally got up and dressed, leaving her in bed, he looked at the watch on his wrist and saw that it was a quarter to twelve. He went downstairs and sat under the little trellised arbour at the back of the hotel and ordered coffee. While waiting for it to arrive he found a telephone directory and started to look for the number of the shipping agency down in the port, only to discover that he couldn't remember its name. It was only when Madame Vlasopulos came back with his coffee and bread and honey and ripe figs that she was able to tell him what it was.

He wrote the number down in his diary and went on with his breakfast. The day promised to be as hot as ever and the first mouthfuls of steaming coffee made him sweat. Thunder had done little or nothing to clear the air, which had the same glueiness as the day before, and there wasn't a single stir of breeze off the sea.

When he at last went to call the shipping agency it was a quarter past twelve and there was a great jumbled crackling on the line. No distinguishable word came out of it at all and three times he replaced the receiver and started all over again. Then it occurred to him that it was past midday and that the office would be closed for another two hours or more and in a mood of listless resignation rather than real frustration he gave it all up and went out into the little square and stood on the harbour wall, staring at the sea.

A boat was passing. Something familiar about its squat white shape stirred a memory and he saw that it was the same boat that had once passed his bungalow, with the two men and two women aboard. Now only the two men were aboard and when he waved a hand to them he got a friendly wave in reply.

Idly he watched the boat tie up some distance down the harbour. The sun beat fiercely on the top of his bare head and this in turn made him remember something else. Far from getting used to the sun he seemed to feel the excessively dry power of it more acutely every day. For some time he had been telling himself it would be prudent to buy a hat and after watching the white boat a little longer he strolled across the square to where, under a big indigo umbrella, a woman was selling scarves and straw hats and shells and belts and souvenirs.

After trying on several hats he finally chose a mottled pink and blue straw with a blue band that he thought looked rather gay. The woman, sucking a large red iced lolly on a stick from one hand, laughed as he put the hat on and then gave him a square black-framed mirror with the other.

He grimaced into the mirror and she laughed again, holding up her thumb. He grinned and held up his thumb too and then, in the mirror, caught sight of the reflection of something that made him turn sharply with astonishment.

There, on the far side of the square, he saw his

second familiar sight of the morning: the old, reckless, windowless tourist bus that had taken him fruitlessly up to the temple on the day Ruth Forbes had arrived. It needed no blast of a whistle to confirm this but a moment later one split the air, to be followed sharply by two others, and he saw the unmistakable figure of the female Greek guide, the sergeant-major, night-capped as before, marshalling her tourist ranks before departure.

'Is everyone not here?' he heard her say with a piercing accusation that carried clearly across the square. The customary desperate counting of heads began. 'We should be twenty-three. No. Twenty-one. *Vingt-et-un. Ein und zwanzig.* Someone is not here. Seventeen, eighteen, nineteen, twenty. One is missing. Who is not here?'

Amusement and curiosity made him walk across the square. Six or seven people hadn't yet climbed into the bus; the rest were sitting inside it with something of the doleful air of soldiers about to be drafted to service in foreign parts.

The sergeant-major climbed into the bus too and again a furious counting of heads began. Precipitously she almost fell out again and immediately blasted the air with a treble accusatory blast of the football whistle.

Jack Marsden was a mere fifteen yards away when her keen pursuant eye detected him. She hurried towards him across the square, white night-cap furiously bobbing.

'Are you with us? We are ready to depart. I can't remember if you are with us or not.'

He deemed it a good moment to take off his new hat; and did so, a trifle mockingly.

'No, madam. Not this time.'

'Oh! it's you. The Englishman. Clearly you are not with us. I remember you ran away from us. You are not very interested in our great culture.'

'It's the heights,' he said. 'I can't stand the heights.'

'You missed the Sacred Lake. There are no heights there.'

'Water makes me giddy.'

'We are going to the Sacred Lake now. Immediately. You may join us if you wish. Seventy-five *drachmas*.'

'No, thank you.'

He laughed; and she found it distasteful.

'To come to Greece and not see the great riches of our culture is quite incomprehensible.' She withered him with a stare of thin-lipped acidity. 'But then you are English. Perhaps you are like Lord Elgin. You are only here to steal.'

She turned abruptly, almost soldier-fashion, and marched back to the bus. From there he heard several voices call:

'He's here now. Everybody's here now. He'd gone to buy cigarettes.'

'These delays are very annoying. In future persons must only buy things at the recognised purchasing places. Otherwise the schedule cannot be kept. Good! We depart now!'

At a final blast of the whistle the bus moved off. Jack Marsden strolled across the square, putting his hat on, and then walked under the arcades on the far side of it, out of the sun. The bus did a complete circle of the square and came back, passing him as he stood in the shade.

As he did so he saw his third familiar sight of the morning. It was Mrs Keller, sitting on the back seat of the bus.

And as the bus disappeared he could almost have sworn that she had seen him too.

In a mood of intensely conflicting emotions, nervousness, frustration, sheer anger, a cold helplessness and something very like fear, he went upstairs to his bedroom. Anger made him throw his hat on to the bed. It fell off and he kicked it savagely like a football.

Then he lay down on the bed, trying to get his thoughts straight and clear. He felt as if the sun had drugged him. It was like being presented with some highly complicated mathematical problem when three parts drunk and told that you have two minutes to give a cold clear answer. After a time he found it utterly impossible to get any kind of clarity into his thoughts and he got up and walked up and down the bedroom, beating one hand into another. A savage disposition to call Mrs Keller every evil name he could think died from sheer impotency and he could only pace about, muttering:

'Christ Jesus, Christ Jesus, Christ Almighty—'

Then, knowing that somehow or other he had to put on a face of calmness before finding Ruth Forbes again, he washed in cold water, brushed his hair and finally felt a little better. He even had, he thought, to go one better than calmness. The day had begun jauntily, with the sort of indulgent banter that lovers delight in so much, and somehow he felt he had to recapture the mood.

The hat, he thought, might help him. He would joke about the hat. He would grimace when he wore it. He would wear it at an angle, jauntily, or on the back of his head.

In her bedroom Ruth Forbes was dressing. She was still in her slip and was sitting on the bed, brushing her hair. He went into her room with a bounce, the hat on the back of his head, and she greeted him with a solemn stare.

'Sorry I've been a long time—'

'I never saw anyone look less sorry.'

'It was the 'phone. Darling, I've been trying all this time to get the agency—'

'You promised to come back to me and you didn't. I don't like you any more. Why did you buy that awful hat?'

'I started to feel the sun rather a lot out there on the square—'

'On the square? I thought you'd been telephoning all this time?'

He started to feel all his uncertainties and frustrations crowding back. He stopped the attempt at banter and said:

'I'm sorry you don't like the hat. I rather thought you would.'

'Oh! it's a hat.'

He went and sat on the bed beside her and put his lips on her bare shoulder.

'Seriously, darling, I've got to get the agency somehow. If I don't get an answer after lunch I'll have to drive down there and fix things up. We've got to get that boat.'

'Is it so desperate? The boats never seem awfully full.'

'I didn't say it was desperate. I want to get you home. To England. That's all.'

All his mind started crying to him that it was desperate; he had to get her out of here, quickly and for keeps. In this rush of desperation he actually thought for one moment of telling her the bare, unpleasant and simple truth about what he had seen – that like an odious ghost from an evil mortuary Mrs Keller was not only back but had seen him too – but he lacked the confidence in himself rather than the courage to do so.

'I could use a drink,' he said. 'I expect you could too. Let's have some lunch and then I'll deal with the agency.'

'Eating again. Nothing but thoughts of eating.'

He made a sudden attempt at light-heartedness and with a laugh fondly ruffled his hand into the nest of hair at the back of her neck.

'Would it help if I kissed your breasts again?'

She smiled, putting her mouth against his ear.

'You could try.'

Then he made still another attempt to be light-hearted and with a laugh said:

'Shall I tell you something?'

'Only if it's the truth. I've a funny idea I don't get much of it from you, you seducer.'

'The day I first met you I thought perhaps they couldn't be real.'

'How very flattering. So that's what you've really been trying to discover about me all this time?'

'Exactly.'

'You false-hearted monster. And do they now come up to your expectations? Are they real enough for you?'

'I love them. They're very real and very beautiful.'

In this more relaxed mood they finally went down to the arbour for lunch. A drink did a good deal to restore his confidence, so that at least he presented an appearance of outward calm. He even succeeded for a time in putting Mrs Keller out of his mind and after a second drink even got as far as telling himself that perhaps after all she hadn't seen him standing there. Or, even if she had, she hadn't recognised him in the hat. The hat, perhaps, was part of a providential pattern after all.

As they ate lunch she said:

'While you were out there flirting with the girl on the ice-cream barrow or whatever it was you were doing I was thinking of England again. What are you going to take me to see when we get there?'

He ignored the reference to the ice-cream barrow, glad of an interlude when he could talk of something far away.

'Is it so terribly, terribly green, as everyone says it is?'

'Pretty green. Wonderfully green sometimes. What would you like to see? – all the things Americans like to see? The Tower of London, Hampton Court, Anne Hathaway's birthplace, Runnymede and all that—'

'I've a longing to go to a pub and drink beer and learn to play darts.'

'That's easy. And where would you like to be married?'

'It isn't possible to be married in a pub I suppose?'

'Hardly think so. At the same time we're not short of churches.'

She was eating a salad of dressed cucumber; she raised a slice or two of cucumber with her fork and then forgot it for fully half a minute and stared abruptly away into far distances.

'I'd like to be married in some small church in a small place somewhere in the country. Nobody else there. Nobody but you and me. That's one of the things I've loved so much about being here – there being nobody else. The isolation. I've never known such lovely isolation.'

Abruptly he remembered Mrs Keller. He too had been aware of the lovely isolation. He was desperate that nothing should break it now.

'And how many children would you like to have?'

An odd look came over her face. Not quite complexity, not definite enough for embarrassment, it reminded him of the way she had looked several times on the morning he had first met her. For the first time for several days she looked uncertain of herself, and at the same time almost enigmatical.

Immediately he started bantering again:

'I had it in mind we might perhaps have ten or a dozen. They're cheaper by the dozen.'

'How charming. And which of them do you propose to bear?'

'It's my job to create,' he said, 'not suffer the consequences.'

'You monster!'

She aimed a swift and playful blow at his head, catching him across the ear, just as Madame Vlasopulos brought a basket of fresh fruit to the table. He laughed loudly and Madame Vlasopulos, her body shaking like a jelly as her big dark eyes rolled, laughed too.

When Madame Vlasopulos had departed, leaving the basket of fresh peaches, pears, figs, apples and grapes spread on new vine leaves in the centre of the table, the girl said in a whisper:

'She knows we slept together last night. After you'd gone out this morning she came in to make the bed and found me sitting manicuring my nails, without a stitch on. She gave me a very long look and grinned.'

'With disapproval?'

'Oh! no, with obvious envy.'

He laughed again. Another drink or two of wine before he picked his first fig from the fruit basket raised the level of his optimism so much that he was again on the verge of telling himself that Mrs Keller was a myth. She really hadn't been there after all.

A few moments later Madame Vlasopulos came back with two little brass finger-bowls of fresh water, giving him a special side-long glance as she set them on the table. He gave her a slow glance of his own in return. The girl was quick to notice it and said when Madame Vlasopulos had departed again:

'I didn't miss that. Just you be careful. So far I haven't seen a Mister Vlasopulos around.'

'I'm always careful.'

'My foot. Flirting, eating, drinking and luring girls on to islands are the least of your vices.' She suddenly dropped a bunch of small black grapes into her finger-bowl. Many small white pearls immediately formed on the gleaming skins, so that they looked as if dipped in grains of sugar. Then she swirled them gently to and fro in the water and then, on the swiftest impulse, reached across the table and put her hand on his. 'Oh! I love you so much. You're so awfully good for me.'

A great tenderness towards her melted all his veins. He simply sat looking directly into her eyes, so momentarily overcome that he didn't even see the brown-gold pebble veins that always fascinated him so much but only the entire bright well of the pupils, moist with tears of happiness.

'Don't look at me too long like that,' she said. 'I shan't be able to bear it if you do.'

'Nor me. So you be careful too.'

For some time after this they didn't speak much; the need for talk was no longer there. Slowly he peeled himself a fig and after washing two others in the finger-bowl simply left them where they were. He couldn't remember a single day in his entire life when he had been so happy or when happiness had had such a specially profound or moving quality. He found himself exulting in an isolation mystical as well as tender, totally oblivious of other people eating under the arbour or of Madame Vlasopulos at last bringing the coffee.

He was finally aroused from this trance by the girl saying:

'I think Madame Vlasopulos would like to know if you're having something with your coffee.'

'No thanks. I won't really.'

He looked up out of his isolated entrancement to see that Madame Vlasopulos had set a tray of bottles on the table and was eyeing him with side-long enquiry.

'Oh! do. It'll improve your siesta.'

'Oh! are we having a siesta? I thought we ought to go down and contact the agency—'

'I know a girl who needs one very badly.'

She smiled and once again he was caught up in

a pure trance of happiness, hardly aware of what liqueur he was choosing for his coffee or that Madame Vlasopulos had poured it and departed. And then, hardly knowing what he was saying either, he picked first an apple, then a peach and then a pear from the basket and said:

'The fruit all looks so beautiful, the colours are all so wonderful, and yet it never ripens. It just matures and that's all. No juice, no anything. Only the figs are really any good. Look at this peach — it looks a dream but in fact it's as hard as hell. Hard as old Keller.'

Driven by some curious reflex of his mind the words were out before he could stop them. He saw her give a quick, unhappy start. Her eyes involuntarily widened and she said:

'Whatever made you say a thing like that?'

'God knows. Search me.'

She seemed about to say something and then suddenly stopped.

'I certainly wasn't thinking of the old faggot,' he said. 'Damn her. Let her rot.'

The strong overtones of indifference completely failed to impress her. She looked down at the few remains of the pearly grapes in her finger-bowl and he swore at himself inwardly several times for being all sorts of a fool. Then as if she wanted to make quite sure in her own mind of something she said:

'You didn't go out for any special reason this morning, did you?'

'No. Just to telephone the agency, that's all. Why?'

'Nothing. I didn't think you were really with me, that's all.'

Her suspicions troubled him; he could suddenly find nothing sensible or convincing to say. He sipped his coffee, which was cold by now, and played with the brown grains at the bottom of the cup, stirring them with his spoon.

'If it's that little ice-cream girl getting under your skin,' she suddenly said, 'I'll strangle the little wretch.'

He found himself able to laugh and to his delight she laughed too.

'There isn't any ice-cream girl. It's a man with large black moustaches. And the only girl under my skin is you.'

'You know just how to melt me, you monster,' she said and again her eyes were moist with near-tears of happiness, moving him greatly for the second time. 'You really do.'

They slept, naked for coolness and outside the coverlets of her bed, until five o'clock. He woke first and she only a few minutes later and he said:

'Would you like a glass of mint tea? Or something like that?'

163

'No, thanks. I suppose if we're going down to this agency we ought to go. What I'd love most is a swim. Can't you telephone?'

'We'll have to go down anyway sometime to fill in the papers. It might just as well be now. We've only one more day and you said you'd like to picnic for the last time then. We can swim tonight. We haven't had a night swim for a long time.'

They took the car and drove back into the port. The small white ship with the chicory blue band across her funnel lay tied up at the quayside, along which the usual crowd of donkeys, mules, idlers, mothers and babies, ice-cream sellers, porters and bicycle lovers jostled and ran.

He parked the Ford beyond the little café where he and the girl had sat drinking coffee the first morning they had met; and then the two of them walked back to the agency.

'Yes, sir, we *hope* the *Patria* will sail on Sunday.'

'You hope?'

'She is having more engine trouble, sir. But it is supremely certain she will be ready.'

'All right. Can you give me two berths?'

'To Athens, sir? I think so, sir. Names please?'

He stood at the counter with the girl at his side, preparing to fill in a number of forms which the shipping clerk pushed across to him.

'I'll do yours first,' he said to her. 'You never told me your full name.'

'Barbara Constance Virginia—'

He had hardly started to write her name when a familiar blast from the football whistle rang shrilly across the quay outside. He felt all his veins go cold and turned sharply to see the reckless, windowless bus pulled up thirty yards away. A sudden fear of Mrs Keller prompted him to an action so quick that even the girl, this time, wasn't suspicious.

'Blast, my pen's run dry again. It's the heat I suppose. It's always running dry in the heat.'

'Here is a pen, sir.'

'Oh! don't bother,' the girl said. 'I've got mine. I'll fill them both in. I'm used to it. I must have filled in a million this year.'

She started to fill in the forms and he walked over to the window and stood looking out. Marshalled by the night-capped sergeant-major, the bus-load of tourists, sun-spectacled, camera-heavy, guides and brochures held like prayer books, was disgorging on to the quayside.

As always, the counting of heads was going on and now he found himself counting them too, waiting tensely for Mrs Keller. He counted steadily and with care until the bus was completely empty and then realised, to his infinite relief and astonishment, that Mrs Keller was no longer among them.

The incredible realisation that he must have been mistaken after all made him go quickly out on to the quayside. He walked ten or fifteen yards towards the ship, searching the faces of the tourist platoon as he went and counting yet again. A renewed blast of the whistle caused the platoon to turn ship-wards and again like a party of soldiers departing for foreign service they started to file up the gang-way. Again he searched their faces and for the third time counted them one by one, but Mrs Keller still wasn't among them.

After the last of the tourists and the shepherding sergeant-major had disappeared on to the deck of the ship he went back with a sense of infinite relief to the shipping office.

'Oh! here you are. Where did you suddenly rush off to?'

'Oh! it was just the woman I call the sergeant-major. The tourist guide. I told you about her. I just went to watch her go aboard.'

'No doubt with the object of kissing her good-bye.'

'Of course. It was the fondest farewell you ever saw.'

She smiled and said the forms were finished now. The clerk took them, glanced down them and then said:

'And where are you staying, sir? Just in case there is some change.' Jack Marsden told him. 'Thank you, sir. Otherwise it will be eleven o'clock on Sunday.'

'You mean morning, I take it?'

'Morning sir, yes. Report here at ten.'

That night, when it finally got dark, they took the car and drove about a mile along the shore. There was no moon by this time but the stars were many and of great brilliance in a deep blue-black sky. They undressed on the beach. The air was still oppressively warm but there was no thunder and no breath of wind on the sea.

They swam naked. This, she told him several times was the only way to swim. She had always heard that and now she knew.

'Now I know what it is to feel absolutely free,' she said. 'Like I said before. Absolutely isolated. Do you feel that too?'

He said Yes, he felt like that too. She floated on her back and said:

'Like when you're a child and you play hide-and-seek and you find the perfect hiding place and you know no one will ever find you.'

For him there was something momentarily almost heartbreaking about the way she said this but his own sense of exultation, returning again and again as he thought with relief of Mrs Keller, drove it quickly from his mind. Without a word he caught up with her where she floated, gently rested his hands on her shoulders and swam, pushing her across the dark face of the sea.

'Only tomorrow,' his mind kept telling him. 'Only tomorrow now.'

# 12

They slept late again. It was after eleven o'clock when he at last got out of bed, peered through the shutters at the morning glare outside and said:

'What about breakfast? I could ask Madame Vlasopulos to bring some up.'

'No breakfast, thank you.'

'I think I must have some,' he said and then paused. 'On second thoughts I don't think I will. The coffee made me terribly hot yesterday. I'll go and get myself an ice-cream.'

'And you have the indecency to tell me she's an old man with big black moustaches.'

'The moustaches are a disguise,' he said, 'just to fool jealous American tourists.'

'I won't let you go. Come back here into bed with me. There's a great gap in here when you go.'

'Meek as a lamb,' he said and quietly slipped back into bed with her.

'That was a lovely swim we had last night,' she said, 'under all those wonderful stars. Shall we do that again?'

'Yes,' he said. 'Tonight. For the last time.'

When he at last got up, half an hour later, she reminded him:

'Don't forget to speak to Madame Vlasopulos about the picnic when you go down. Otherwise it doesn't give her much time.'

'The picnic was all arranged yesterday. Madame is doing something rather special for us, as it's the last time.'

'No doubt seduced into it by you.'

'No: she suggested it all herself. We're going to have cold *Kebab* and *Pilaff* and bread and cream cheese and stuffed vine leaves and honey cakes and fruit and lots and lots of wine.'

'Sounds wonderful. She's been very sweet to us.'

He finished dressing, put on his new hat and went downstairs. In the lobby he met Madame Vlasopulos, who said:

'Good morning. The picnic is quite ready when you are. Everything is ready. Do you like to have breakfast?'

He thanked her and said no, he wouldn't have breakfast.

'Very well. Just tell me when you are ready for the picnic. All is ready.'

The morning sun was hot and powerful as ever.

It still seemed a good idea to buy himself an ice-cream and he walked along under the arcades to where the man with big black moustaches sold all sorts of them, mostly on sticks, from plummiest purple to pale lime green. He chose himself a plain vanilla one and stood for some minutes in the shade, idly licking the ice and staring out at the sea. Presently the white boat passed, juttering slowly through the harbour, with the two men in it, but they were too far away for him to wave.

Soon an old-fashioned looking black taxi drove into the square and drew up in the centre of it and he stood idly watching that too. Then the driver, in a white peaked cap, got out of it and immediately after him a woman in beige slacks, who stood for a moment or two in the glare of sun, her face turned to the sea. Then she turned round and stared at the Hotel Acacia and he saw in a moment who it was.

It was Mrs Keller.

She started to walk towards the hotel. His mind immediately began raging and the impetus of it took him in ten or a dozen long quick strides across the square so that in only a few seconds he stood in front of her.

'What in hell are you doing here? What do you want, Mrs Keller?'

'I might ask you the same question.'

'What I am doing here is my own business. It's no concern of other people.'

'So? Then why get so het-up and rude about it?'

Mrs Keller's eyes had the same eely, oily look in them as ever; but now, he thought, they seemed altogether colder. The look in them was more compressed. She too looked as if she hadn't slept well for weeks. Big smoky, unhealthy bags had formed under her eyes, throwing up into uneasy relief the almost dead-looking pupils.

'Go back to the taxi,' he said. He felt by no means cold himself. Sweat was running down his forehead, pouring freely over his eyebrows and into his eyes. 'Go on. Get out of here.'

'Will you move out of my way? I wish to see Ruth.'

'Ruth? What Ruth? Oh! her – by God, I thought she went up to Brindisi with you weeks ago.'

'How do you know she went to Brindisi?' The over-large mouth oozed its melting smears of orange lip-stick; the squarish nostrils quivered contemptuously. 'You lied to me over the telephone, didn't you? Of course she was staying at the *Helios*. I'm staying there myself. I've seen the hotel register.'

'You stinking bitch—!'

'I also happen to know that she's staying here

at the *Acacia*. They told me so at the shipping agency.'

'By God!—'

He raged incoherently, half aware that he was making a complete fool of himself and yet unable to do a single thing about it. He resisted an insane impulse to strangle Mrs Keller where she stood and then she said, in that guttural voice of hers and in a bloodless sort of way that enraged him more than ever:

'Will you let me come past, please? It won't take long to settle things.'

'Settle things? There's nothing to settle. It's all settled, I tell you.'

'What do you mean exactly? Settled?'

He gripped the stick of his ice-cream violently, waving it in front of her face like some impossible dagger.

'She's going to marry me. That's what's settled, see?'

Her face went several degrees whiter; her tongue came out, almost adder-fashion, licked swiftly across her lips and shot stiffly back again.

'I never heard such nonsense in my life. She's not the marrying type. She never would.'

'We're engaged,' he said. 'Get that into your head.' His voice was much lower now. 'We're going to England. We leave by the *Patria* on Sunday.'

173

She gave the most odious of smiles at this and said:

'It so happens the *Patria* doesn't sail on Sunday. She doesn't leave till Monday now. I shall be on her too.'

He suddenly felt his entire world cracking about him as if some sort of intangible and awful earthquake had undermined it. Completely beside himself, he waved the ice-cream and its stick in front of her, again like a dagger, and shouted:

'If you don't get back into that blasted taxi in half a minute I'll ram this down your throat. You poisonous bitch, I'll choke you!'

In the face of all this she remained quite inhumanly calm. The high Teutonic cheek-bones stood out like arrogant bastions of fleshless bone. Only the nostrils quivered repulsively again.

'Ruth will be coming back with me,' she said. 'I've only to talk to her and she'll understand.'

'You'll talk to her over my dead body.'

'I don't think so. I don't think you quite appreciate that she has certain obligations.'

'Obligations? For Christ's sake, what obligations?'

In answer she said something so insanely and wildly impossible that he felt he had suddenly been hit by a bolt from heaven.

'Our child,' she said, 'for one thing.'

'Your what?' he shouted.

'Yes, we have a child.' He felt all his senses roll and sicken. 'It's a boy.' He felt himself suddenly to be a half-deaf lunatic, not hearing properly. 'We adopted it in Southern Italy.'

He stood impotently in the sun, sweating, sick, unable to think of a single word to say.

'If the adoption is a success we shall adopt another. And perhaps even another and then bring up the whole family on my farm.' All this time she spoke with the same unspeakably inhuman calm, as if reading off facts from a mechanical computer, and he stood impotently half-listening, his anger drained. 'Now you see why I say she has obligations. We have both signed the necessary papers. It's a thing she has to go through with. I think she may have forgotten that. And that's why I say I think she'll see my point of view when I talk to her.'

Jesus, he thought, I'm not here. I'm in some crazy loony bin for the damned. The mad gods have got at me—

'Still,' Mrs Keller said, 'we needn't worry too much longer about that. Because here she is, coming now.'

He came to his senses with a sickening gasp. He turned sharply and saw Ruth Forbes coming out of the hotel. She smiled and then stopped completely. The look of blank shock on her face made her suddenly appear, as she had done on that first morning on the *San Philippa*, a figure of pitiful loneliness. She simply stood there helpless in the sun and then he ran across to her.

'Go back to your room,' he said. 'Lock yourself in and stay there.'

She didn't say a word; she looked limp and cold and frightened and almost mesmerised even at that distance, he thought, by Mrs Keller's stare.

'Don't talk to her,' he said. 'She's going to try to make you go back with her. She's going to do everything in her bloody awful power to make you.'

Suddenly she looked limp and helpless no longer; she drew a great deep breath and it seemed to stiffen her.

'I'm going to talk to her.'

Before he could do or say anything she was walking over to Mrs Keller. He followed her, feeling utterly helpless now himself. Then the two women were facing each other and Mrs Keller said:

'Ruth, I want to talk to you.'

He stood for a moment petrified by what her answer might be; and then with the beginnings of an amazed joy he heard her say quite calmly:

'There's nothing you have to say to me, Beatrice, that means anything to me any longer.'

'I think it will when you listen.'

'It means nothing to me any longer.'

'Please listen to me, Ruth.'

'My name isn't Ruth, either.'

Now there was sweat on Mrs Keller's face; he saw it running down copiously, smearing her lips with an orange oil.

'I merely want to remind you,' Mrs Keller said and for the first time the voice was quite unsteady, 'that you have certain obligations. There is the child. You undertook the obligations and you have to face up to them. Ruth, I want you to come back with me.'

'It means nothing to me any longer.'

'Ruth, you're coming back with me. You're coming back with me if I have to go to the ends of the earth to make you do it.'

The girl took another deep breath. All this time he hadn't said a word; now he suddenly felt like shouting in another burst of overjoyed amazement.

'Beatrice,' she said, 'I haven't forgotten that you tried to kill me.'

Mrs Keller stood speechless, utterly still, neither the oily eyes nor the big square nostrils moving now.

'If you don't go now,' Ruth said, 'I'll go back to the Consulate in Brindisi and tell them all about you and what happened.'

Mrs Keller seemed about to speak. But all she

gave was an abrupt guttural sort of cough of rage and for a second the tongue flashed out adder-like again. Then she turned and walked sharply back to the taxi.

Without a moment's hesitation he seized the girl's arm and took her back to the hotel. A rather concerned Madame Vlasopulos met them in the lobby, wondering about the delay in starting off for the picnic, and said, looking at the girl:

'You look rather sick. Are you all right? Is something the matter?'

'She's just seen the devil,' he said. 'We both need a brandy – big ones,' and Madame Vlasopulos went away to fetch them herself.

In the arbour under the acacias the girl alternately sipped brandy and sat with her head in her hands, silent from utter exhaustion and relief. He didn't speak much either. He merely said once that he knew how difficult it had been. His spent anger had left him dazed and curiously unvindictive. He was merely glad that it was over.

And then as his brain began to work again he remembered something. He remembered how the *Patria* wouldn't, after all, be sailing on Sunday. He remembered too that when it did sail Mrs Keller would be on it and once again all his fears and misgivings came crowding back on him.

Then in desperation, after more brandy, he remembered something else. He remembered the conversation he had had with his friend the sad, talkative waiter on his first morning at the *Helios* and he recalled at the same time the white boat that so often sailed into the harbour with friendly waving hands.

'I'm just going out for a moment,' he said. 'I won't be more than ten minutes or so.'

'Oh! don't leave me here. Not at this moment, please.'

'I'll ask Madame Vlasopulos to come and talk to you. I won't be a quarter of an hour.'

'Why do you have to go now? Why just now?' She managed to raise the shadow of a smile. 'Not the ice-cream girl again, surely?'

He explained, at the same time smoothing her hair with one hand.

'The *Patria* doesn't sail on Sunday. She goes on Monday now. Mrs Keller told me. She'll be on it too. There must be some other way of getting off this damned island.'

He was back in less than half an hour, half-inarticulate with relief and excitement.

'There's a man with a boat – a small motor cruiser,' he said. 'You must have seen him go past. He'll take us across the straits tomorrow to that little town where we can see the lights at night. It'll take three hours or so. We can go at six in the morning and then get the bus to Athens.'

'Thank God for that,' she said.

# 13

After some time she recovered her nerve, finished her brandy and then confessed, rather sadly, that she was afraid she wouldn't be able to make the picnic after all. He wasn't surprised by this and went with the news to Madame Vlasopulos.

'Oh! no, please.' Madame Vlasopulos, sad too, looked desolate. 'I make such nice food for you. The *Kebabs* will be wonderful. The cheese came just fresh this morning. Oh! why can't you go?'

He explained that the morning had been rather a hard one for Miss Forbes. She was under an exceptional strain. She had a headache and felt she didn't want to eat at all. It was all too bad but—

'But the air will do her good. It is always bad here in the town, so low down by the sea. It's a bad situation here for headaches.'

Another thing, he said, it was rather late now and it was a long way to go.

'Oh?' she said. 'Which way did you plan to go? How far away?'

He began to explain and she threw up her podgy hands in instant protest.

'Oh! there is no need to go so far for a good place. There is a most wonderful place here, just at the back of the town. One mile. It's where the stream comes down. You will like it. You have only to go along the street here as far as the fish-market and then turn left. Then you go up by the church with the big bell and after that the road forks. You take the left fork and then you can hear the stream.'

He hesitated, in something of a dilemma, not knowing what to say.

'Oh! please eat my nice food. And the wine – I put in something very special. You can put it in the stream to cool. It will do her good to drink lots of nice cool wine.'

'All right. I'll see.'

'Good, good. You will find it better. It will be terribly hot down here this afternoon.'

He went back to the girl who, when he had explained, said:

'All right. I feel rather better now. And I'd just hate to hurt her feelings. She's been so sweet to us.'

'Good. I really think it would break her heart if we didn't go.'

It was nearly two o'clock when they drove up

the narrow road, steep and white between crumbling walls of stone, out of the town. The church with the big bell dominated, out of all proportion, the last squat flat-roofed houses of the town and after that there was no sign of habitation to break the great steps of yellow rock, harshly fissured, and the sweeps of olive, acacia, myrtle and pine. The roots of the bigger trees clung to the rocks like gnarled claws and a white dust blew from the wheels of the car and floated away to settle on fierce slopes of windless leaves.

They decided to picnic on a flat space of rock, a few yards above the stream, under a big evergreen oak so dense with leaf that the shade of it was almost black. The sound of water leaping down over rocks drove an entirely new beat into the chorus of cicadas, who seemed to fight hysterically to be heard above it. All the heat of the day sang and shimmered out of the cicadas' endless clamour but the stream had a cold, eternal sound.

The water was actually cold too and he put the two bottles of wine under a rock to cool while he helped the girl to unpack the rest of the picnic. He protested once that he could well do all this himself, while she rested, but she said:

'I like doing it. I'll feel better if I do.' And then: 'The sound of falling water is a marvellous thing when you haven't heard it for a long time. I think

I must really go and wash my hands and face in that water before we start to eat.'

'Do,' he said. 'You'll feel fresher for that. I might even dabble my own feet in it later.'

He watched her bending over the stream, dipping her hands in and out of the water and occasionally lapping it over her face. He felt enormously proud of her at that moment and every now and then new and unexpected waves of tenderness went flowing warmly through him. It wouldn't be long now, he kept telling himself; it was all as nearly over now as it could be. There was a finality about that speechless departure of Mrs Keller's on the square that, fantastic and repugnant though the episode had been, struck him as almost pathetic. For a brief moment he reconjured for himself an image of the sick eel-like eyes and felt, incredibly, almost sorry for her, all vindictiveness and rage at last completely burned out inside him.

The girl came back to him refreshed and actually smiling. He had already poured her a glass of wine which she hadn't touched and now he went over to the stream for the rest of the bottle. It was already quite cold to his touch and he said:

'Drink a little. Then I'll fill up your glass. It's beautifully cold already.'

She drank; he lifted his glass too and said:

'Well, here's to tomorrow.'

'Tomorrow,' she said, 'and to England.'

At first as they began to eat they talked very little; there was no single word between them of Mrs Keller; the episode on the square was the end of an act neither of them wanted to recall or discuss again. When he spoke he contented himself with sudden bursts of enthusiasm:

'By Gosh, these *Kebabs* are good. Simply marvellous. Madame Vlasopulos was right. I've never had them cold before. They're really jolly good.'

'They certainly are jolly good,' she said. 'Everything's jolly good.'

It made him laugh to hear her say this; it made him feel that she was already free and happy again. But it pleased him even more when, as he bit into the first of the honey cakes, she said:

'Tell me some more about England. What's it like in the Spring? You always hear about England in the springtime.'

In a leisurely sort of way, in disjointed phrases, he started to put together for her, like a jig-saw puzzle, a picture of England in the Spring. He thought first that she ought to see the primroses, whole woods of them and countless hedgerows, and with them crowds of white anemones. And then the cherry orchards, black branches, huge festoons of snowy flower. Sometimes, in good years, all the orchards came in a mad rush to bloom

together, pear and plum and cherry and apple,
and then the millions of bluebells, all the woods
smoky purple, and thick with them.

'My God, I'm getting quite carried away,
aren't I?' he said. 'Is this a bore – the Englishman
raving about his native land?'

'I love it. Tell me some more. What's really the
best time?'

'About the end of May,' he said. 'Then it's like
a great big anthem being sung, with all the stops
out. Madness everywhere. Blackbirds, nightin-
gales, thrushes, God knows what, all clamouring
away together in terrific chorus—'

Suddenly he felt himself to be no longer on a
parched Greek hillside, where the rare sound of
falling water could induce a strange and unexpected pleasure, but back in a landscape of
flowering wood and meadow, with oaks in bloom,
and hawthorn, and rooks nesting high in emerald
beeches.

'There's a place I'll take you, on a hill of big
beeches, where bluebells flower by the million.
I'll show you the very same view the Romans
saw—'

He broke off, suddenly uneasy. He thought he
saw a quick shadow of something moving across a
rock beyond the fringe of black oak shade. It
might have been the flight of a bird, he thought at
first, and then he turned sharply and saw,

standing in an open space of hillside, not thirty yards away, Mrs Keller.

She had the revolver in her hand. Before he could do anything she started slowly to walk forward. For a moment or two he was stunned into complete impotence by the shock of seeing her there and then his senses came rushing back. He lugged the girl to her feet, pushed her farther into the shade and shouted:

'Run! For Jesus Christ's sake, run! Run! – anywhere.'

He heard her crashing through the undergrowth. He picked up a rock. With extraordinary calmness he found himself thinking 'She can never hit me from that distance. Even a good shot couldn't hit me from that distance. You couldn't even hit a barn door.'

In the same instant she fired for the first time. The shot was very wild, missing him by several yards, and in return he threw the rock. That missed too and he shouted:

'Put that bloody thing down and get out of here! Do you want to kill somebody? I suppose it's me this time?'

'Yes, it's you,' she said.

'How in hell did you know we were up here?' he shouted.

'I told you I was very good at finding out things, didn't I?'

He remembered dear, sweet Madame Vlaso-pulos and all his rage came rushing back. He picked up another rock. He bent his arm in the act of throwing it and at the same moment she fired a second time. The rock seemed to leave his hand of its own volition and a second later he felt the bullet whip clean across his knuckles like the belt of a whip. He yelled with pain and looked down to see the four fingers of his right hand strapped together by a wet band of blood.

She was still walking slowly towards him and as he watched her, his hand dripping blood on to his shoes, the whole affair became like a brighter, more ghoulish version of his dream. Then he had desperately wanted to run but couldn't; and all of a sudden he seemed to hear the voice of the sad-faced waiter urging him to run.

'By God, he was right,' he said to himself. 'It's the wise ones who run. This is sheer bravado. This is plain bloody silly. I'll get myself killed if I stay here and then she'll have the pair of us—'

He turned suddenly and ran back fast into the shade of the oak and started to clamber wildly up the rough path that bordered the stream. She fired a third time as he ran and then a fourth as he started to climb.

After that it was completely quiet again. It was perhaps five minutes before he found the girl, shaking and white and desperately quiet too, pressed up against the trunk of a pine some fifty yards up the hillside. She didn't speak at all as he put his arms round her to try to comfort and calm her and all he could think of to say himself was:

'I'm beginning to think there's some sort of curse on us both. I'm beginning to think we're never going to get out of here.'

Then she saw his hand; she cried out in sick terror as she saw it, starting to weep, and said they must get him to the stream.

'No. Just bind my handkerchief round it. We'll have to wait a bit. She can't have gone yet. She's still waiting down there somewhere.'

They waited too. She bound his fingers with the handkerchief. The hand had started to pain him considerably by now and in an effort to numb it he stuffed it hard into the pocket of his shorts. She had the presence of mind to say:

'No, no. Keep it up. You've got to keep it up. Put it in your shirt – hold it there.'

He stood there more frustrated than angry now, irked by the need for waiting. The great noise of cicadas and the sound of falling water, mingling together, seemed to make the entire hillside shake with a peculiar frenzy. The girl stood shaking too, saying at last:

'She might have killed you. She might have killed you.'

'That's exactly what she came to do.'

'I feel terrible. I can't bear this much longer.'

'Fortunately I don't think she's all that good a shot—'

Even as he said the word a fifth shot rang out from lower down the hillside. Startled into sudden clarity of mind again, he was surprised to hear no ricochet. Only the echo of the shot went prancing and whining up the rocks and in and out and back again.

It seemed like half an hour before he left the girl and walked back down the path. He stopped for a few moments by the stream lower down, searching the rocks ahead. Then he went on and saw the picnic things as they had left them. One of the wine bottles, kicked over, had spilled red across the rock. A few black ants were already coagulating on a piece of broken honey cake. A piece of white cheese lay like a squashed wet rose in a pool of wine.

It was some time before he found Mrs Keller. She was lying a considerable distance further down the stream. The red hole in her face, above the too high Teutonic-looking cheek-bones, and the long ribbon of blood reaching down to her neck seemed to make her, if anything, more odiously mocking than ever. For several moments he stared blindly down at the dead face and then at last he slowly covered it with his hat.

Exhausted, he dragged himself with pain up

the hillside. He stopped once to wash his good hand in the stream and splash a little water over his face. When he finally went on and reached the girl he found her flopped at the foot of the pine, crying as if her heart would break, with hardly the strength to support her head in her hands.

He let her cry for some time longer and then he finally stooped and took her by the shoulders, gently, and lifted her up.

'I thought you were never coming,' she said. 'I thought—'

'It's no time for thinking,' he said. 'Come on. We've got to get going now.'

'What kept you so long? What happened? Where is she?'

He started to walk with her down the hillside. Everywhere the chorus of cicadas beat at him with delirious unreality. Like warm balm the scent of myrtle filled him with slow comfort.

'She's with the gods,' he said. 'The gods have taken her.'